William Hurrell Mallock

The Heart of Life

Vol. I

William Hurrell Mallock

The Heart of Life
Vol. I

ISBN/EAN: 9783744728904

Printed in Europe, USA, Canada, Australia, Japan

Cover: Foto ©Andreas Hilbeck / pixelio.de

More available books at **www.hansebooks.com**

THE
HEART OF LIFE.

BY

W. H. MALLOCK.

IN THREE VOLUMES.

VOL. I.

LONDON: CHAPMAN & HALL, Ld.
1895.

THE HEART OF LIFE.

CHAPTER I.

ENGLAND, in spite of railways, still has a few districts which remain, for various reasons, almost as remote and primitive as they were a hundred or even two hundred years ago. Of such survivals there is no more complete example than that afforded by a part of Devon and Somerset, which consists mainly of bleak and mountainous moorland, and confronts for some thirty miles the waters of the Bristol Channel. It is true that here and there amongst its unvisited valleys lonely populations hide themselves in villages with surrounding hedgerows; and in some of the valleys also, streams, brown with peat, slide and pour and foam through cloisters of sequestered woodland. But of spots like these a stranger sees nothing ; and even here, in the green glades, or by the farm or by the village mill, there is a sense in the air of the open surrounding country— of rolling hills, bare to the wind and mist, where the tufted heather lifts itself, solitary as a wave at sea.

Geographically, however, civilization is not far off. On the western frontier of this region is the well-known watering-place, Lyncombe, its wooded crags and hillsides glittering with hotels and lodging-houses ; and on the eastern, a shed at the end of a straggling hamlet forms the terminus of a branch line of railway. But between these two points the progressive world of to-day shows its existence only in a modern road connecting them, and even this looks nearly as wild as the solitudes through which it passes. So at least it may well strike a stranger. The coast, from which it is rarely more than half a mile distant, is the loftiest in all Great Britain, reaching in many places a height of twelve hundred feet ; and the timid traveller, as he is driven over these elevations, is apt to feel dizzy at the sight of the monstrous precipices to which he constantly fancies that his wheels will approach

too near; whilst inland his eyes meet nothing
but a world of gorse and heather, bounded
only by clouds brooding on the distant tors.

Along this road, during the summer, daily
once each way, a tawdry coach rattles, generally top-heavy with tourists; but these incongruous apparitions pass, leaving no trace
behind them, except perhaps some fragments
of drifting paper; and by the time the dust
raised by their transit has subsided all that
stirs in the landscape is the fleece of some
moving sheep. A stranger, indeed, might
look about him during the whole journey and
detect no sign of human occupation anywhere
except some stretches of dry stone wall,
which at certain places appear, skirting the
road, and accentuate rather than relieve the
solitary aspect of the scene.

Nowhere do these walls produce this forlorn effect upon the mind more strongly than
at a point about eight miles out from
Lyncombe, where the road, after a long and
rugged climb from the sea-level, reaches at
last a high and wind-swept down, which is
bare of everything but boulders and stunted
grass. What could be the need of any enclosure here is a question that well might
baffle the passing curiosity of the traveller;

for the land on one side would hardly attract
a donkey; and on the other, after fifty yards
or so, it appears to tumble into the sea. But
a still more perplexing feature is a gate in the
seaward wall, carefully painted white, and
giving access to a fragment of open road,
which to all appearances leads only to the
brink of an adjacent precipice. By this gate
also, as if to enhance its mystery, a solitary
figure used always to be seen standing every
afternoon on which the coach passed from
Lyncombe—the figure of a lad, roughly but
not ill-dressed, who received daily a leather
letter-bag from the driver, and disappeared
with it over the brow of the cliff, as unaccountably as if he had been changed there
into a sea-gull.

A stranger following him would eventually
have encountered a sight almost as unexpected as he would have done had this
miracle actually happened. For on gaining
what, as viewed from the coach, appears to
be a cliff's edge, he would have seen before
him an amphitheatre of steep slopes, down
which, by a feat of great engineering skill,
the road was led in a long succession of
zigzags till it reached in the depths below
a belt of feathering pine woods. Descending

it thus far he would have found what was invisible from above—a pair of gate-posts surmounted by moss-grown griffins, a lodge with latticed windows almost hidden amongst the branches, and an iron gate guarding the entrance to a gravelled drive. Resuming his course within, the intruder would have been surprised to perceive that his way, which now lay in a green and sheltering twilight, and was bordered by slanting carpets of moss and of ground-ivy, still continued to descend, zigzagging much as heretofore ; and the sea as it shimmered in occasional vignettes through the trees, would have shown him that still it was hundreds of feet under him.   At length, however, after he had walked for a good half-hour, certain signs would have assured him that he was nearing the end of his explorations.   His eyes would have been caught by a glimpse of slate roofs ; and, the road dividing itself in a thicket of rhododendrons, he would have seen that one branch of it led to some stable buildings, whilst the other would have brought him to an open balustraded space, with the waves breaking a hundred feet below ; and with a house on one side of it, whose stucco turrets and

chimneys betrayed the Gothic taste which
flourished at the beginning of the century.
It was indeed like a Tudor mansion, as the
contemporaries of Beckford conceived of one,
reduced in all its details to the scale of a
good-sized villa.

The bad taste of a bygone period mellows
with years, as associations lay their tints on
it; and this sham Gothic architecture, in
addition to its picturesque outlines, has for
our generation the charm of an historic
pathos; speaking as it does of an England
which is now completely vanished, but
which yet, through the pictures retained by
us of the grandparents who were surviving
in our childhood, almost seems to touch
some nerve in our own memories—the un-
reformed England of chariots and post-
chaises, and the eyes, the necks, and the
guitars painted by Sir Thomas Lawrence.
And in the case of the present building, the
effect of its own aspect was heightened by
the beauty and the singular character of its
situation, as it stood with its drawing-room
windows opening on a terrace of garden,
where two peacocks were accustomed to sun
themselves on the stone parapet, and with
the woods rising behind it till they seemed to

meet the sky, except where some higher rock came peering over the pine-plumes like a cloud.

But up to a date that is still comparatively recent, the life that was lived in this retreat was more curious than the place itself. For inside the arched and nail-studded front door, and the fantastic multiplicity of windows, what survived till the year 188— was the end of the last century, rather than the beginning of this. No sooner was a visitor admitted to the entrance hall than the spirit of that period was puffed into his nostrils like a scent, breathing from beeswaxed floors, from china bowls and vases, from busts on marble tables, and from old Turkey carpets. The past is often associated with decay and dust; but it was not so here. Everything, on the contrary, was as fresh and sweet as lavender. The oak floors were like glass; the china shone with cleanliness; the flowered and faded chintzes were all newly calendered. Only the chairs and sofas were such as Miss Burney or the Miss Berrys might have sat upon; and of the books which filled, with their glimmer of gilt calf, the many shelves, or loaded the square whatnots, few were more modern than the earliest editions of "Childe Harold."

One broad impression this interior would have at once conveyed to a visitor—that the villa appertained to a family of which it was not the principal seat. In the drawing-room was a beautiful Sir Joshua, and there were two Opies in a breakfast parlour; and these, which were the only large portraits visible, had all the air of having a tribe of companions elsewhere. Again, there were certain articles of furniture, remarkable though not numerous, such as one or two large and fine pieces of buhl, and a rose-strewn Axminster carpet, faded and soft like moss, which seemed as if originally they had belonged to some statelier home. And that such was the case was rendered none the less probable by the different kind of evidence supplied by some smaller pictures—miniatures and oval pastels, which spoke of connections with an obsolete world of fashion; several of the former representing well-known beauties of the Regency, and two of the latter bearing, on their gilt frames, the information that they were gifts of the Prince Regent.

But between these mementoes of royalty hung something yet more interesting—a pastel also—the portrait of a lady in a turban, in the full regard of whose melting and melancholy eyes all the romance floated that troubled the days of Byron. Small as this picture was, it filled the air with sentiment, like a faint perfume from some single living flower. There were traces, too, on all sides, of devotion to art and literature. Art, indeed, was represented chiefly by such fragments of the antique—bronzes and marble busts— as a hundred years ago men of taste used to bring from Italy ; but the book-shelves, in addition to their fortuitous multitudes of "Spectators" and "Elegant Extracts," "Tom Joneses " and " British Theatres," contained a collection of volumes whose character and whose sumptuous bindings suggested that they had been got together by some one remarkable man—a scholar, a dilettante, and a philosopher, as well as a lover of luxury.

There were other things, however, fraught with very different suggestions. Amongst the gilded leather bindings which filled most of the shelves, and not far from the neighbourhood of a fine copy of the " Decameron," were several rows of works by the Tractarian divines of Oxford — such as Pusey, Keble, and Newman — in all the holy poverty of their original cloth backs. On the walls, moreover, were mezzotints of several of these divines themselves; and, as if to explain their presence, some cases containing scissors and knitting-needles—prim little dainty cases made of shagreen and tortoise-shell—were carefully arranged, like relics, on certain small mahogany tables; whilst displayed symmetrically between two pairs of silver snuffers was a book of family prayers, with a purple marker hanging from it. Here were signs of the presence, and also of the will, of some woman; and a certain formality in the neatness and disposition of everything bespoke the presiding genius of an old maid or a widow.

Both these sets of suggestions accorded with actual facts. The villa, which was known by the romantic appellation of Glenlynn, had, at the recent date to which reference has been already made, been occupied for sixty years by a certain old Miss Pole, who was then on the point of reaching her hundredth birthday. The Poles had from early times been a considerable landed family. Pole Park, which they had enlarged in the reign of George II., enjoyed the reputation of being the longest house in ——shire; and they had contributed to the world of fashion dandies, sportsmen, and politicians, whose figures had been familiar at White's, at Almack's, and at Newmarket. But these fashionable successes were now things of the past; and the family had, for more than fifty years, been almost unknown in London, though it continued to flourish in the country. Such knowledge of it as remained in the mind of the world in general was due to the fame of one of its bygone members—Tristram Pole, the wit, the scholar, the exquisite; who was remembered less for the qualities which, when he was seven-and-twenty, had made the Prince Regent call him the best bred man in England, than for a tragic and unfortunate love affair which brought his brilliant youth to a close, which inspired a beautiful but unpublished poem of Byron's, and left him to the day of his death a changed and a solitary man.

He it was who, shutting up Pole Park, had built Glenlynn on a remote fragment of his property; and except for occasional journeyings in Greece, Italy, and the East, he had there spent in seclusion the latter part of his life.

On his death, at fifty, his estates passed to

a brother, with the exception of Glenlynn, which he left to his one unmarried sister. This lady, who at the time was close on the age of forty, though possessed of a fortune which had commanded much male affection, had never been tempted to renounce the single state. Delicate health in her girlhood, and a religious turn of mind, had combined to keep her at home, and to prevent her mixing in society. She had, indeed, lived little out of her own county; but first at Pole Park, and afterwards at a neighbouring dower-house, she had been a far greater lady than she ever would have been in London. She had been the Providence of the cottager, the patroness of the rector, the confidant of deans and bishops. Her third brother, who had inherited a good estate from an uncle, was one of the archdeacons of the diocese, a man of great talents and accomplishments— a horseman, a magistrate, an artist, a fellow of All Souls, an incumbent of five livings, and a believer in Apostolic Succession. Through constant association with this dig- nified churchman, Miss Pole had found an opening for her benevolence and her talents for management; and had early acquired a taste, which never afterwards left her, for the respect, the deferent sympathy, and the conversation of the superior clergy. When she removed to Glenlynn, at the mature age which has been mentioned, she not only continued, in that comparative isolation, to organize the distribution of soup and blankets amongst the poor, but devout and cultivated divines, whose manners had been formed at Eton, were her frequent guests, with their neckcloths and old-world faces, and read prayers for her, and praised and appreciated her Madeira.

As years went on, however, these passed, with their generation, and their place as High Churchmen was taken by the sacerdotal revivalists of Oxford. In one respect, and in one only, Miss Pole marched with the times; she sympathized with the Oxford Movement. She began to talk of the Church, oftener than of the Church of England; she admired Archbishop Laud; she read the "Lives of the Saints"; she bought silk book-markers with brass crosses at the end of them; and she opened her doors to a new circle of clerics—eager and active men who rejoiced in being described as priests. But except for this exhibition of spiritual or intellectual progress, Miss Pole's ideas and habits underwent hardly any change. To the day of her death her views as to the constitution of Society, the humility incumbent on the poor, the importance of county families, the ignoble nature of trade, and the wickedness of the French Revolution, were the views of her class at the end of the last century; whilst her establishment and the appointments of her house were survivals of its domestic economy. On the dining-room sideboard the knives were ranged in their old knife-boxes, and the bright-patterned cups and saucers, and sparkling Georgian silver, made her breakfast-table look like an old picture by Gilray.

But Miss Pole's own personal breakfast-table, at the date which now concerns us, had been for many years nowhere but at her own bedside; and she had been visible to her guests or dependants only at certain hours, when her housekeeper, or an old companion, herself verging on decrepitude, introduced the visitor to an audience in an upstairs parlour. On such occasions Miss Pole was invariably found sitting bolt upright in a comfortless straight-backed chair, her face framed in a cap, her hands covered by black silk mittens, and her glass of midday port, and a volume of Keble's sermons, usually standing on the heavy table close to her. Her voice came like a tremulous echo from a cavern; but her intelligence was as clear, and her questions were as shrewd as ever. Each day's post brought her a large budget of letters, some containing news, but most of them requests for charity; and two hours daily were spent by her in dictating answers to them, except when her doctor, the primæval practitioner of Lyncombe, forbade her to exert herself, and wrote her a new prescription.

But one August day, the tourists on the Lyncombe coach, crossing the high downs with the heathery wind in their faces, heard blown at intervals up from some unseen valley, the sound of a tolling bell; and on inquiring of the driver what this mystical sound was, they learnt, for the first time, probably, that such a lady as Miss Pole had existed, by receiving the news that she was dead.

CHAPTER II.

THE exterior of Glenlynn that day bore witness to what had occurred within. All its windows were masses of down-drawn blind, whose whiteness made the discoloured stucco yellower. It was five in the afternoon. The sun was glittering on the chimneys frilled with their toy battlements, and was populating the pine-woods behind them with shadows like inverted arrow-heads. A scent of mignonette came faintly from the garden; but no sound was heard except the occasional scream of a peacock; nor was there any movement except the flash of its blue breast.

Suddenly this silence was broken by hoofs and wheels, and there drove up to the Gothic front-door a good-looking waggonette and pair, having a large-bearded man in it. He descended slowly, with the peculiar air of one who feels that the smallest action is significant when he himself performs it; and

before ringing the bell he stood and contemplated the house, like a statue of Dignity
culminating in a bust of Beneficence. A
square of clerical collar which glimmered in
the shadow of his beard was hardly needed
to proclaim the fact that he was a clergyman.
His wide-awake hat itself was eloquent of
Anglican orders, and his waistcoat was a
manifesto of his belief in their sacerdotal
virtue ; whilst a loose jacket, in place of the
long conventional coat, quietly indicated a
chastened amity with the world.

"Gibbs, my good man," he said, turning
slowly to the coachman, "I fear it is all over."
And he laid his hand on the iron knob of the
bell-pull as if he were blessing the head of
a little child.

Presently the door was opened by an old
man in white stockings and faded green knee-
breeches—a footman old enough to have been
the father of many butlers. The visitor
scrutinized him, and in a voice that was like
a cathedral echo, he gave utterance to the one
word "John!" It was a simple word in
itself, but as uttered now, it vibrated with
every meaning that was most proper to the
occasion. It was inquiry, human sympathy,
and religious consolation in one. The old

man understood it, and looking gratefully at the speaker, he whispered, "She passed away, sir, at nine o'clock this morning." His withered lips twitched, and pressing his hand to his eyes, he shrank instinctively back into the shadow to hide himself.

Fortunately for him, however, this unconventional retreat was covered by the advent of an odd little squat woman, who at this moment came waddling out to the doorway. Her forehead was crossed by a thin black velvet band, and her face flanked by bunches of corkscrew curls, like a couple of nosegays tied to a horse's blinkers. This was Miss Drake, the late Miss Pole's companion, who had driven with her, sat with her, read to her, and written her letters; had made tea for her guests at breakfast, and judiciously absented herself from dinner, with hardly the break of a week, for the past forty years.

"Oh, Mr. Godolphin, is that you?" she exclaimed, grief and asthma wheezing amongst her syllables. "We thought you were still in Scotland. Of course you have heard what's 'appened." She was by no means without aspirates, but when she was hurried or agitated she would drop one, now

and then, much as she might have dropped
her pocket-handkerchief.

"I *have* heard," Mr. Godolphin answered. His manner was as kind to her as
it had been to the old footman ; but it was
more majestic, as to one who could appre-
ciate majesty ; and her left shoulder coming
within easy reach of him, he laid his hand
on it in a way which made him appear
to be wrapping comfort round her, like one
of his own great coats. "We must remember," he said, "that our sorrow is only for
ourselves, not her. Blessed are the dead
that die in the Lord, for they rest from their
labours, and their works do follow them."

Mr. Godolphin's voice, which had as many
tones in it as an harmonium, seemed to have
concentrated into these last words an entire
religious service. Then for a moment he
was silent ; but when he began to speak
again, his manner, though still solemn,
underwent the same change that it did every
Sunday when he emerged from his own
church door and exchanged with his parishioners in the churchyard observations about
the crops and weather. Having paid a due
tribute to the profundity of Miss Drake's
grief, he sought to lessen its strain by

asking her as to the details connected with it.

In simple cases, he was an excellent spiritual doctor; and by putting these questions he produced the relief desired. Miss Drake at once became more or less mistress of herself, and in another moment she was not only coherent but voluble.

"Her end," she cried, "was like a child falling asleep; and Dr Clitheroe gave her the 'oly sacrament. Canon Bulman, as you of course know, has been called away for a week, and only came back this morning; but we've had the Doctor with us, it must be now for a fortnight; and he's been so good and tender, and prayed by Miss Pole's bedside, and helped her about her business—her earthly business as well as her 'eavenly, as if he'd been born a lawyer. Mrs. William Pole—she's here too, and has been this last month; and her son, Mr. Reginald—you can't have seen him for years—he's been telegraphed for. He was coming back to England anyhow from Berlin, or Russia, or Lisbon—I'm sure I forget which; and dear Miss Pole thought she would like to see him. Telegrams were sent to him at I don't know how many places, so as to catch him on his way; but only the last reached him, and now he'll arrive too late. We expect him to-night. We hoped he'd have been here this morning. But, Mr. Godolphin," said Miss Drake, suddenly wiping her eyes with a wrinkled finger which had three mourning rings on it, "won't you step in and take just a cup of tea? Mrs. Pole is busy; and as for me—I'm so helpless, I feel all in a dream. I feel, I assure you, as if I were dead, not Miss Pole. But the Doctor, I'm certain, would be very glad to speak to you. I saw him a minute ago pass out into the garden."

"Let me," said Mr. Godolphin, with an obeisance, "go into the garden and find him. I won't detain you. God bless you, Miss Drake, and good-bye. To-morrow I will send over and inquire if I can be of any assistance. My house, my carriage, my horses, are all at Mrs. Pole's disposal." And he waved an apostolic hand in the direction of his prosperous equipage.

The Rev. Sunderland Godolphin was a man happy in the double consciousness of valid priestly orders and three thousand a year. His comparative wealth, however, produced no vulgar pride in him. It was for

him merely a sort of mental magnifying
glass, through which he saw the sanctity of
his own sacerdotal office. He was, and had
been, for some twelve years, incumbent of a
moorland parish, the living of which was in
Miss Pole's gift, and in which his generosity
had been new every morning. Having long
since rebuilt both the church and schools, he
was at last treating himself to a billiard-room
for the benefit of his boy who was at Harrow.
Whilst this was in progress, he had indulged
in a two months' holiday, and his duties
meanwhile had been taken by Canon Bulman, whom Miss Pole, for that period,
had accommodated at Glenlynn as her
guest.

Mr. Godolphin's inner being, when he
turned from the front door, was full of a
melancholy, yet not unhappy, activity. He
heard his own voice reading Miss Pole's
funeral service ; he saw himself bareheaded,
advancing to meet her coffin ; and he felt
that one among the many fitnesses of her
death would be his own resonant accents
consigning her to her final rest. His broad
chest was expanding and straining his waistcoat buttons, and tears were preparing to
mount to his handsome eyes, as he passed

through the gate into the small Italian garden, whose carpet of bright flowers glittered before the blinded windows.

His solitary emotions, however, had not time to complete themselves, for he saw at once, in a corner of this enclosure, something black and motionless, which he recognized as Dr. Clitheroe. The Doctor was short, and had just a hint of portliness. Mr. Godolphin's waistcoat was expanded across the chest; the Doctor's emulated it, but a little lower down. He wore a long full-skirted coat, and a tall silk hat, which was badly brushed, and very broad in the brim; and his general appearance suggested that a mere touch would transform him into a dean. He was hardly more than fifty; there was a quiet alertness in his eyes; and his lips were elongated into a placid and kindly smile, which lost itself in cheeks slightly pitted with the small-pox. In his own way the Doctor was an eminent man. He was not beneficed, but he held an important post under Government, and had now been deputed to visit various parts of the country, in order to draw up reports for a Royal Commission on Education.

"Ah, Doctor!" exclaimed Mr. Godolphin,

his voice running before him, like a courier dressed in mourning.

The little Doctor turned himself round promptly; with short steps he trotted to meet the visitor, and the two were presently walking side by side. A series of remarks were naturally exchanged between them, respecting the excellence of the deceased, and her painless and hopeful death. Dr. Clitheroe's gentle accents were peculiarly suited to the theme. At last, however, with an access of finished briskness, he turned from the death itself to certain matters connected with it.

"Of course," he said, "you know that for her life Mrs. William Pole has everything; and that after her death it goes to Mr. Reginald Pole, her son. About this, I suppose, there never was any secret. His father, I have understood, was Miss Pole's favourite nephew; and as for the son, Miss Pole, on the father's death, paid for him at Eton and Oxford, and made him an allowance since, which his mother will of course continue. As for himself——" The Doctor smiled and paused. "Perhaps," he said, "I ought not to talk of these private matters. By the way, I suppose they have told you of Miss Pole's wishes about the funeral. She especially desired to be buried in the church at Earlsbury, in the same vault as Mr. Tristram Pole, her brother."

To Mr. Godolphin this news was a thunder-bolt out of a clear sky. It made him feel as if Miss Pole had unexpectedly died again. For Earlsbury was not his parish; and to add to this defect in it, its church had never been restored in accordance with modern ideas; its old clergyman was in a condition analogous to that of his church; and it seemed to Mr. Godolphin that the solemn rites he had been contemplating were sud-denly emptied of their choicest and their most comforting elements. Dr. Clitheroe, however, was altogether unconscious of the dreadful desolation he had spread over his companion's mind, and continued talking in the same meditative voice.

"I can't imagine," he said, "what they will do here for accommodation; so many relations most likely will want to attend the funeral."

"My dear Doctor," said Mr. Godolphin, rousing himself, "you and Canon Bulman must come and stay with me. I will send my carriage for you at any moment that suits you.   I could take you now, if you like."

"I," the Doctor answered, "am going to the home farm.   I sent there this morning, and found I could have a bedroom.   I know, however, the Canon intended to ask you for hospitality; but he wishes to remain here for a couple of nights, if possible, so as to see Mr. Reginald Pole, to whom he was once tutor.   Look—here the Canon is."

A dark figure, pushing aside a blind, had at this moment emerged from one of the drawing-room windows, and with a rapid directness advanced towards Mr. Godolphin, greeting him from a distance with a smile full of gleaming teeth.   Canon Bulman had all the air of a sanguine and strenuous traveller on the road of duty, of hard work, and of preferment.   His complexion was fresh; his clothes were of the finest cloth.   From his watch-chain there dangled a heavy, though plain, gold cross, a miniature compass, and a pencil-case in the shape of a cricket-bat.   He carried his chin high.   His large broad lips had, in repose, the appearance of being clenched like a fist, and there was on his face a certain expression of belligerence, like that of a man playing football

against the devil. He grasped Mr. Godolphin's hand with a dry, business-like vigour,
and the three clergymen began slowly to
pace one of the walks together.

"I was sorry, Godolphin," said the Canon,
when he had first honoured the occasion by
referring to Miss Pole's death in a voice of
prosperous sorrow, "I was sorry that I was
called away; but I suppose you know the
reason. I was called to speak, indeed, take
the chair, at two meetings, convened for the
purpose of declaring, at this momentous
crisis, that private purity on the part of
public men is, to the nation, even more important than their politics."

It had lately happened that the leader of a
powerful Parliamentary party had increased
his fame by appearing as co-respondent in a
divorce case; and Canon Bulman, who previously had been one of his chief admirers,
was the first clergyman belonging to the
Established Church to demand that the
bestial sensualist — the infamous domestic
traitor — should resign his seat, and be
hounded from public life. Chastity, in fact,
was the Canon's favourite virtue; so much
so, that many who respected him for his
earnest efforts to promote it, almost felt that

he accorded it an invidious preference over the others, especially when he ventured to declare in a well-known pulpit at Oxford that the story of the woman taken in adultery was spurious, on the ground that it conflicted with the entire spirit of Christianity.

The two other clergymen, as any observer might have perceived, were considerably milder in disposition. Indeed, a shadow of pain passed over Mr. Godolphin's face. He said, however, taking the Canon's arm—

"I know that the cause of right has no more ardent soldier than yourself."

"Lord Shropshire and Lord Wakefield," continued the Canon, "both spoke at my meetings, and admirably, too—quite admirably. Wakefield was staying with me—one of the finest fellows I know. By the way, since we happen to be talking of other things, I confess I can't help regretting that she, who has just left us, did not desire some other place of burial."

Mr. Godolphin was delighted at the conversation taking this turn, and hastened to echo a sentiment with which he so deeply sympathized.

"I confess," he said, "I regret it, too."

"It seems," the Canon resumed, with dry and trenchant emphasis, "regrettable that one whose life was so eminently Christian, should weaken the force of her example by thus wishing to rejoin a man who caused, in his own day, the same kind of hateful scandal as that which is shocking the public conscience now."

This was a very different utterance from what Mr. Godolphin had expected, and neither he nor Dr. Clitheroe knew how to receive it. They were, therefore, both of them not a little delighted at a sudden interruption supplied by a startling sound. It was the sound of a steam whistle; and, so far as their ears could inform them, it rose from the waters directly beneath the garden. The three clergymen made their movements accordingly; and before long, when they had reached a lower level, they distinguished against the waves some films of ascending smoke. Canon Bulman, who was a renowned Alpine climber, raised himself on a spike of rock, and looked curiously over.

"A launch!" he exclaimed; "a beautiful little private launch! There is nobody in it except the engineer and a sailor."

"I hope," said Dr. Clitheroe, "that on a day like this the place will not be flooded by any intruding strangers."

They had reached, as he spoke, a spot where the path divided, one limb of it, like a gutter, scrambling down to the sea, the other leading up again in the direction of the house and garden. Here Canon Bulman suddenly started forward. He stooped to the ground and raised from it some light, pale-coloured object. It was a woman's grey glove, delicate and slightly scented.

"It seems," he said, holding it out to his companions, "that strangers of some sort must be in the grounds already, though not —I should judge from this—a party of rough excursionists. Hush—listen! People are there above us." To confirm his observation, a few loosened pebbles, just as his voice ceased, rattled down the upward path, and a second later the nervous form of a woman appeared round a corner, descending on a pair of rickety boots. The woman's dress was black, and *piquante* with French neatness; but her face, though not unpleasant, was very far from distinguished, and a metallic exclamation of "*Oh, mon Dieu !*" occasioned by a sight of the clergymen, and by a simultaneous slip of her heels, would to any experienced ears have explained her as a Parisian maid. Canon Bulman, however, being no discerner of persons—or, to speak more charitably—no respecter of them, with much *empressement* offered her a hand to assist her, and tendering the glove to her, said, "I think this must be yours." But before the young woman was able to return a suitable answer, another presence had come into sight behind her—a woman also, but one of a very different aspect. About her, too, was a something suggestive of France, not England—a certain simple yet fastidious neatness of dress, which in the present scene looked exotic; but her movements and the poise of her figure differed from those of the other as the figure of one of Watteau's shepherdesses might differ from a Dutch doll. She was evidently quite young, but too self-possessed to be girlish. Her mouth carried in its curves a certain imperious sadness, and the lights in her eyes were like jewels on dim velvet. Canon Bulman gazed hard at her, wondering why he did so. He noticed a pearl at her throat, and one in each ear also. He raised his wide-awake hat, gripping it by the limp crown.

"Could you," she said, in a voice that was at once soft and crisp, "tell me the way to the house? Ah! my glove. How good of you! I knew I had dropped it." And she took it from him with a hand dainty as Dresden china.

"Do you want to go to Glenlynn?" asked the Canon, with grave deference.

"Yes," she answered, "to inquire after Miss Pole. We heard she was ill. I have come by sea from Lyncombe."

"She died this morning," said the Canon simply. "If you went to the house, I fear you would see no one. Mrs. Pole is very busy. Would you allow me to leave a message for you?"

"Will you? I should be indeed obliged to you. I have a letter for Mrs. Pole." And she drew, from the pocket of her jacket, an envelope, which she gave the Canon. "I am sorry," she went on, "to hear what you tell me; though I myself never knew Miss Pole, nor saw her."

The Canon cleared his throat. "I," he said, "am only an accidental guest here; but I am sure I shall be doing right if I ask you to have some tea."

"You are too kind," she replied, drawing

on her glove as she spoke. "But I could not have waited in any case. It is late. I am much obliged to you. Mrs. Pole will know from the letter who I am. Clarisse—come; we must go back to the boat."

"Allow me," said the Canon, "to assist you down this terribly steep path."

The young lady declined the offer with the prettiest grace imaginable; but the Canon's chivalry was much too vigorous to be repulsed; and a moment later he was disappearing between some rocks and rosemary-bushes, with the hand of the fair stranger supporting itself on his broad shoulder.

"He's a good man," sighed Mr. Godolphin, looking after him; "but not always discreet."

Dr. Clitheroe smiled, as though conscious of a little worldly knowledge. "It's a pity," he said, "that the Canon, who is so alive to a certain kind of evil, should not always detect it, when it is present in his own household. I was told at Windsor, that one of his parlour-maids—a pretty girl of the name of Sophie—is the scandal of the place, owing to the way in which she conducts herself; and that the Canon, when the truth has been represented to him, indignantly

refuses to believe it.   Men of his eager
temperament are frequently taken in by
women.''

A minute or two later the Canon was
visible re-ascending, wearing on his face a
consciousness of successful gallantry, and
yet, together with this, the irritation of some
puzzled thought.   '' That's curious,'' he said,
'' most curious ! I mean that young woman's
face.   It's quite familiar to me.   Where—
now where can I have seen it ?   It's not a
pleasant face.   No, no, no—not pleasant.''

'' The Pole connection,'' said Mr. Godolphin, magnificently, '' is immense, as you,
Canon, who live so much in the world, know.
In all probability you will hear she is some
relation ; and you may perhaps have met her
yourself at a State Concert.   Did you ever,
by the way, see Mr. Pole, the head of the
family ?   The last of the squires they call
him.   He is sure to attend the funeral.   And
the Duke ''—Mr. Godolphin had much simple
reverence for high rank, and he pronounced
the name of the Lord Lieutenant of the
county as if the mere utterance of it was an
honour to himself—'' the Duke, who is a
relation also, and full of all right feeling, will
be present most likely— indeed, I should say,

certainly. It will be an impressive gathering, if only the service itself could be performed with more seemliness."

The Canon, whose devotion to democratic principles, was only equalled by his taste for aristocratic persons, listened to this information with much smiling attention; but unfortunately the concluding words touched a different part of him.

"You remind me," he said, "of what I remarked just now. The larger this gathering is to be, the more sincerely I deplore the fact that Miss Pole should have elected to be buried by the side of her adulterous brother. Had I," continued the Canon, "known that such was her wish, I would have frankly told her what I feel about it. I was, in fact, just before my departure, on the point of remonstrating with her on a very similar subject. You both, perhaps, can guess what I refer to."

Mr. Godolphin shook his head. "I refer," the Canon continued, "to something you must be well acquainted with—the picture of a woman which hangs here in the first drawing-room. I have often looked at it for a quarter of an hour together, disagreeably impressed by it; but it was only last week

that, by accident, I learnt whom it represented—the shameless partner of the sin of
Miss Pole's own brother. My dear Godolphin, I don't blame Miss Pole herself; but I
do blame her family for not having long ago
urged her to destroy, or at all events to hide
this object; and I shall certainly, at some
fitting season, mention it to my old friend
Reginald."

"We must all honour you," said Mr.
Godolphin, "for the feelings by which you
are actuated. But tell me," he went on,
eagerly changing the subject, "how is
Reginald? Do you ever come across him
now? I call him by his Christian name, but
it is years since I set eyes on him."

"Ah," exclaimed Canon Bulman, "one of
a thousand—he is." And his manner as he
spoke altered and became fresh and breezy
with good fellowship. "I too have not seen
him for years—except at a levée, in the distance, and once at the late Prime Minister's.
But such a good fellow he was — such a
scholar too—so easy to teach and guide! I
sometimes used to fancy he was a little led
away by all that nonsense about birth and
family, and so forth; and like many of these
young aristocrats he was too apt to think

that Society was the world, and that the
world was a playground for himself. But
all that, I fancy, has now passed away. I
always say that it was I who formed his
mind; and that my teaching it was, which,
in due time, brought forth fruit. When he
went abroad first to stay with his cousin
the ambassador, he thought only of amusement — innocent amusement, I grant you;
and, as I often dinned into him, he was apt
to be shamefully extravagant. But sound
teaching tells; and he hadn't been in Berlin
six months, before he had taken to studying
the industrial conditions of Germany, and
was made secretary to our Royal Commission. I gather, too, that this fault of his,
extravagance, has now quite disappeared;
and that he lives with extreme frugality.
Well," continued the Canon, "to have been
living at all these capitals, and have been
received as he has been in all the best
society—it would have been a dangerous life
for some—very, very dangerous. But as for
him, he morally is one of the cleanest men
I know."

These last words were ominous of a return
to his favourite topic; but Mr. Godolphin
interrupted, by exclaiming, "Ha! there are

my horses—look at them—impatient to be off. Whenever you can come to me, Canon, remember, there is your bedroom waiting for you."

They were by this time approaching the front door of the house. Mr. Godolphin turned to his friends, and solemnly said good-bye to them, drawing himself up to his full priestly altitude; and mounting his waggonette, which seemed to become full of him, he vanished to the rapid music of hoofs and of crunching gravel.

CHAPTER III.

REGINALD POLE, whose arrival was that evening expected, and whose character had been described with so much appreciation by his tutor, was the son of a promising diplomat, who, early in his career, had married a distant cousin, and had died in Paris about twelve years afterwards. It proved that his affairs were left by him in extreme disorder; and the mother and her boy would have been in a position of considerable embarrassment if it had not been for the kindness of a certain celebrated Mrs. Steinberg, the wife of a gorgeous banker, who was flourishing under the then Emperor. This lady, true to a constantly expressed friendship, at once offered the two a home for as long as they required one, under the painted ceilings and amongst the ornate candelabra of her hotel; and with her they remained, until, through Miss Pole's aid, the various debts left by

Mr. William Pole were settled. In due time
Miss Pole made known those intentions,
with regard to her great-nephew and his
mother, which were embodied in her will
and testament; and he, as Dr. Clitheroe had
said, was educated and subsequently maintained by her.

Miss Pole, though an admirer and
practiser of all the virtues as she understood them, did not, so far as young men of
position were concerned, include amongst
the virtues any definite work. Diplomacy,
indeed, and the army, she regarded as
channels of temptation; and was inclined to
desire for her heir, when he left Oxford, a
safe career of leisure, which should end in
his being a county member. Little as Miss
Pole had lived in the world herself, she had
always been accustomed to take the great
world solemnly; and she reverenced a duke
almost as much as if he were a church. It
seemed, therefore, to her that one of her heir's
most important duties was thoroughly to
familiarize himself with that distinguished
society which, next to the Church, was a
gentleman's most unerring teacher, and with
which God had been pleased to connect him
by so many ties. He himself, who was full

of social aptitudes, and even more social fastidiousness than he had cared to reveal to Canon Bulman, was not slow to fall in with his great-aunt's views. Such fashionable relations as the Pole family possessed—men and women alike—combined to render his entrance into the society of London easy, and the continuance of this conduct was, in the case of many of them, a personal compliment of which at first he had no suspicion ; being really an evidence less of their own affection for him, than of the credit done by him to the family by his various social talents, which did indeed resemble those ascribed to his renowned great-uncle. On the other hand, much of the welcome which he received from fashionable mothers and their daughters, and which was in reality due to an exaggerated rumour as to his prospects, he was at first simple enough to attribute to a judicious appreciation of himself. Thus his self-esteem was maintained despite his modesty, till in due time he came to understand men and women better, and it was placed on a new basis, which he told himself was knowledge of the world. Meanwhile, however, in addition to the pursuit of fashion, he gave his attention to things of a more serious nature.

He made the acquaintance of certain celebrated men of science, who cashed their drafts on fame occasionally at polite dinner-tables ; and he read their books and discussed theology with them in their laboratories, with results which would have horrified the eclectic freethought of Canon Bulman. He also turned his attention, as Miss Pole had hoped, to politics ; and indeed became gradually intimate with several well-known statesmen.

He was, however, possessed by the opinion, in which his intercourse with these veterans confirmed him, whilst convincing him of its singularity, that accurate knowledge of the life and conditions of nations, the habits of various races, and the details of trade and industry, were almost as necessary to make a member of parliament useful, as experience of the House itself, or a fluency on public platforms. Influenced therefore by this opinion partly, and partly by an unwillingness to sacrifice the delights of freedom, he determined to postpone any effort to thrust himself into public life, until he should have mastered one set of subjects at all events, in a way which should enable him to treat it with some authority. At that time a certain extreme party had begun to proclaim a number of startling doctrines with regard to the poverty and misery of the masses of the British nation, and to demand, on behalf of the poor, who were described as having been wronged for centuries, reforms of the most violent and the most impossible kind. Whilst the majority of practical politicians treated their demands with a smile, the question of fact suggested by them, seized on young Pole's imagination; and he set himself with perseverance, though without exaggerated avidity, to study the condition of the masses as it actually was then, and also as it had been during the past century. It is true that he attempted no personal investigations himself; but he collected with remarkable judgment the most instructive records that were available; and after several years had elapsed, he was at last beginning to think that the time was come when he might gratify his aunt's wishes, and represent the Pole family in Parliament, even if he represented nothing else. He found, however, that to wait for a seat was a very different thing from obtaining one. Amongst seats which were safe for a Conservative, or even hopeful, there were, during eighteen

months only five vacancies; and for these
there were other claimants whose claims
stood higher than his own. Disappointed at
this, though not ungenerously embittered,
he began to think of dismissing his Parliamentary ambition from his mind; whilst a
sense of public duty, which had been growing
in him with the progress of his studies, urged
him, on the other hand, not to shirk his re-
sponsibilities. In this condition his doubts
were unexpectedly solved by a severe illness,
which completely undermined his strength,
and forced him for many years to spend much
of his time abroad.

Amongst other things which reconciled
him to this fate, was the fact of an unfortunate
connection which he had formed with a well-
known demi-mondaine, or rather which she—
a woman of considerable talents—had contrived to form with him. It was a connection
which soon not only wearied but humiliated
him; and he welcomed the circumstances
which brought it rapidly to an end. He took
with him on his travels a portion of his
political library, and still from time to time
he continued his former studies; but new
countries, new societies, the passing excite-
ment of one or two slight romances, and the

spectacle of a new religion, filled his mind
with other thoughts and interests. In Italy
he became acquainted with many distinguished ecclesiastics ; he made a long
retreat in a celebrated Benedictine monastery ;
and his natural revulsion from an amatory
episode unworthy of him, called to life in his
mind that passionate sense of contrition to
which all that is deepest in the Catholic
Church appeals. He was far, indeed, from
becoming a convert to the Catholic faith ;
and, to say the truth, his contrition did not
altogether preserve him from a kind of
conduct which again called for its exercise ;
but on this occasion his heroine was a
complete woman of the world, who first
engaged and then betrayed his affections, and
left him with a wounded heart, as well as a
dejected conscience. Some men by experiences such as these become hardened or
enslaved in vice ; others only learn by them
to see it in a clearer light, and to return with
a manlier understanding to the rules of life
which they had violated. Pole was a man
who belonged to this latter class, partly
owing to a well-balanced mind and tempera-
ment, but still more to the fact that he had in
him, beneath his passions, a capacity and a

need for the affection which passion so often
injures. At all events, the next time that the
personality of a woman appealed to him, which
was not till some years later, the appeal was
of a different kind. He had been staying at
Berlin, on a visit to the British ambassador,
who was related to him; and it so happened
that ust about that time the British Government had undertaken to institute a Royal
Commission, to inquire into the working of
trades unions and the condition of labour on
the Continent. At this, his old interest in
these subjects revived; and his strength by
that time being very nearly restored, he accompanied one of the English officials on
several tours of investigation. On one of
these occasions, a slight attack of illness
detained him for several days in a little
German watering-place; and here, at a table-
d'hôte, he accidentally made the acquaintance of a young Englishwoman and a child,
who were lodging in a house close by. The
mother—or rather, as he presently learnt, the
stepmother—attracted him, not only by her
grace and her gentle beauty, but also by her
forlorn condition, of which he gradually
gathered the details. The head of her
husband's family was a certain Welsh

baronet, who enjoyed an obscure celebrity as the owner of a curious castle. The husband himself, it appeared, was devoted to cards and racing. It was not quite clear to Pole whether he was a jockey or a book-maker. It was evident, however, that he was a great student of economy; for, having heard that this town was the cheapest place in Europe, he had chosen it a month ago as a home for his wife and daughter, till the death of a decrepit relation should enable him, without extravagance, to be as liberal to them as he was to himself.

All this Pole gathered in an indirect way. The wife, he discovered, was also related to a family that was known to him; and this fact, which touched her almost to tears in her loneliness, made her the readier to confide in an unlooked-for friend. A day or two after his first meeting her, his friendly interest in herself was forgotten in concern for her situation. The rent of the apartment she occupied, it appeared, was to be paid monthly, and it now was due, together with a fortnight's bills; but a remittance from her husband, promised her a week back, had not arrived, though she had telegraphed several times for it, and the landlord of her house had already taken to threats which alarmed her all the more because she hardly grasped their meaning. Pole was enabled to discover her sad story only because, on coming one day to call on her, he found her crying into her hands, with her head resting on the table. It was only little by little that he learnt the nature of her embarrassment; and the tears, when he knew the whole, were not in her eyes but his. In another moment, however, he made light of the whole matter, and offered to lend her whatever she might require for the moment.

"On second thoughts," he said, "I will pay it in to your bankers; and when your money comes you can send me a cheque to Berlin."

She was overwhelmed with shyness and gratitude, and, without more words, he left her, naming the sum which she would presently find at her disposal. He had not at the moment more than half that sum in his possession; he did, however, possess a favourite watch, which, not without a pang, he disposed of at half its value. But even this was considerable. He thought of his own expenses in the immediate future; he resolved to reduce these to the smallest amount possible; and then, retaining only what he judged would be thus necessary for him, he placed the entire remainder to his friend's credit at her bankers'. It was a sum which would suffice not only to pay her landlord, but to support her for another month should her remittances be delayed further.

In common with most people, Pole often had heard of want, but he had never before had so vivid an example of it close to him. On returning to Berlin he wrote to the authorities at home, offering, without salary, to take part in the work of the commission. His offer was accepted, his talents being not unknown, and by-and-by he was accorded both a salary and the post of secretary. It was observed by his friends that, either as a cause or a consequence of his work, he rapidly grew in many ways a more serious man than formerly; and that though his income was for the time slightly increased, he emulated in his own life the poverty which he was engaged in studying. He was never, indeed, ill-dressed, nor did he affect ostentatious economies; but it could not escape the notice of those who had known him formerly, that in matters of personal self-indulgence he acted like a poor man.

This self-denial was in part, though not wholly, due to the continued embarrassment of the lady whom he had already assisted. His headquarters for a time were in the little town of her exile; and he often contrived, without her entertaining a suspicion of it, to supplement, through her bankers' agency, the irregular remittances of her husband. The rest of his savings, as time went on, he set aside also for a similarly unselfish purpose. His official work, which enlarged itself far beyond its intended limits, afforded him occupation which lasted for several years; and most of each year he spent accordingly on the Continent.

His work of inquiry was now at last complete, and even had he not had news of Miss Pole's illness, he would, for other reasons, have been returning then to England. The friend whose interests he had taken so much to heart, and for whose sake he had made so many concealed sacrifices, had some months previously been liberated from her German prison. Her husband's pious hopes for the speedy release of his relations had been accomplished by Providence on a more liberal scale than he had anticipated; and he found himself not only in possession of enough ready money to turn his head, and to appease his most pressing creditors, but also of a baronetcy, of a castle, and of a property with appropriate mortgages. Under these circumstances his wife had, in his eyes, acquired a utility which he never expected to find in her; and as a preliminary to settling her as his ornamental housekeeper in the country, he begged her, with a view to producing between him and her enough good humour and amity for the purpose of married comfort, to join him on a tour which he meant to make in America, and which he intended should unite the excitements both of pleasure and of business.

After much hesitation his wife had accepted the proposal, and during her travels Pole had had no news of her. He was accordingly delighted to receive from her, just as he was starting for England, a letter which told him that she had returned, and was staying for a week in London. Most of that week was gone before her letter reached him, but he arrived in London in time to see her for half an hour, though not, indeed, under circumstances that were very favourable to conversation. A note from her was awaiting him

at his club, telling him that she must start
for Wales by a train which left Paddington
in the middle of the afternoon; and she
begged him to meet her at the railway-
station half an hour before. Together with
this letter was a telegram from Glenlynn,
urging him to come with whatever speed he
could; and as the station for both their trains
was the same, the appointment she suggested
was thus easily kept. She was waiting for
him at the door of the booking-office; and,
leaving his luggage with his servant, he
slowly strolled with her up and down an
empty end of the platform, asking her hesita-
ting questions about her welfare and her
immediate prospects. Pole's manner was
naturally not demonstrative; and as for her,
the various replies she made to him were
almost as shy as they might have been had
he been a new and unsympathetic acquaintance. At last, however, when he stood by
her carriage door, and took her hand, just
as the train was moving, her eyes suddenly
filled, and looked at his dim with gratitude;
and she said in trembling accents, " I can
never repay your kindness—all that you
have done for me—or forget it."

" Write to me!" he replied.

" Yes," she said—"yes. Of course I will. But wait till I write to you."

The carriage was already moving. She kissed her hand to him, and she was gone.

His own train started a quarter of an hour afterwards, and, lost in many meditations, he was hardly conscious of the journey, as he was hurried westwards to the house which was thenceforward to be his home.

CHAPTER IV.

MEANWHILE at Glenlynn, the two clerical visitors, having bidden Mr. Godolphin adieu, betook themselves to their respective chambers, where the one copied out a report on workhouse schools with a type-writer, and the other wrote a dozen letters in connection with a forthcoming meeting. Miss Drake was secluded in her own chamber likewise, idle with bewildered sorrow; and though a message was sent to her by Mrs. Pole begging her to be present at dinner, she clung to the custom, invariable during Miss Pole's lifetime, of having her evening meal alone in her own parlour, where a chop and a poached egg proclaimed her loss anew to her, by making her feel how unable she was to swallow them. At the same hour Dr. Clitheroe and the Canon, fresh from their respective labours, were awaiting Mrs. Pole in the drawing-room. Their collars shone in the twilight; their hands were pink with washing; and their lips had the faint cheerfulness that is caused by expectant hunger. Presently Mrs. Pole entered. "Dinner is ready," she said. "Shall we come in? Martin and John have settled that there is to be no bell to-night."

The two old servants stood solemnly by the dining-room door, as the small company passed into a glimmer of light which shadeless candles were casting on silver covers. The dishes were placed on the table as they were a century back; nor, except for such articles as were there for actual use, was there any ornament—not even a single flower. But the plate was fine in its simplicity; the linen was smooth as porcelain; and the ponderous old decanters flashed from a hundred facets.

Mrs. Pole was a woman of charming though faded aspect, which touched those who looked at her like a tranquil day in autumn. In spite of her grey hair, drawn from her forehead artlessly, she seemed to be hardly sixty, although she was really more. A sense of humour was discernible in the play of her features, and there still lived in her eyes the light of some vanished spring-time. The

death of those who die at so great an age
that their life has long been a yearly in-
creasing wonder, can be hardly expected,
except for its accidental results, to break the
hearts even of near relations; and Mrs. Pole
was the last person in the world to put her
voice or her manner into any exaggerated
mourning. She wore, indeed, this evening
the soft veil of solemnity which falls over
most faces in any house of death; but it
subdued her natural smile without affecting
to hide it, and the two clergymen, for her
sake as well as for their own, were relieved
to read in her demeanour a tacit licence to
be themselves. Dr. Clitheroe said to her
cheerfully that he hoped she was not exhausted, and Canon Bulman made apprecia-
tive noises with his soup. Mrs. Pole spoke
in a matter-of-fact voice of the amount of
business that had been forced on her during
the day. "I sent," she said, "a dozen
telegrams in the morning, and more, I
think, have come this afternoon than ever
agitated my aunt in the whole course of
her life." She then mentioned the people
whom she expected at Glenlynn for the
funeral, and the Canon, who wrote articles
against the House of Lords in reviews,

pricked up his ears at the name of a well-known peer.

"That reminds me," he said, wiping his mouth hastily, and plunging his hand into one of his coat-tail pockets, "here is something that I ought to have delivered sooner." And, giving her the letter which had been confided to his care in the garden, he explained the incident, alluded to the young lady's appearance, and watched Mrs. Pole with interest as she broke the envelope open.

"I think," she said placidly, when she had read the letter through, "that I can explain the mystery. Your attractive friend is the daughter of the person who writes this letter, and that person is a sort of cousin of ours. I dare say you know we have certain foreign relations, and this is one of them— Countess O'Keefe, she calls herself. Years ago I met her at Pole Park. She was a regular foreigner in her ways, although she was by birth an Irishwoman. She smoked cigarettes in her bedroom, and never came downstairs till twelve. I need hardly tell you her visit was not repeated. Well, it seems she is at Lyncombe now with a yacht. I suppose if she stays long enough it will be necessary to ask her over."

At the name of O'Keefe Dr. Clitheroe looked up. It was a name at that time celebrated throughout Europe, being borne by a continental statesman who had great influence with his sovereign.

"Has she anything to do," asked the doctor, "with Count O'Keefe, the minister?"

"She belongs to his family," said Mrs. Pole, indifferently, "and so did her husband, for she married her first cousin. She met him at Carlsbad. He was an officer in the Austrian army, and was very rich. His mother was a Polish princess. As for the young lady, I know nothing about her; but the women of that family had all the reputation of being beautiful—of having beautiful figures——"

"This one's figure was beautiful," interrupted the Canon.

"And Reginald heard about one of them," Mrs. Pole continued—"I hope it is not this one—who got into some dreadful trouble. This one's name, as I see by her mother's letter, is Shimna."

The Canon frowned, and listened with grave attention; but the subject dropped, nor was it again approached till Mrs. Pole had departed, and the clergymen drew their chairs together. Then when the Doctor, with a smile like a silent grace, had demurely poured out a glass of old brown sherry, the Canon, who was a total abstainer, helping himself to some French plums, at once went back to the subject of the O'Keefe family, and began to explain a number of facts relating to it, which could not so well have been discussed in Mrs. Pole's presence.

"You did not perhaps know," he said, "that Mrs. Pole was an O'Keefe herself. She was—she was the Dean's daughter: and Count O'Keefe, who is the head of her family, is an Irish peer, a naturalized Austrian subject, and also a Count of the Holy Roman Empire." The Canon, like many a convinced and fierce democrat, was an earnest though secret student of the "Peerage" and "Landed Gentry"; and he proceeded with considerable accuracy to inform the Doctor, how an Irish marquis, Mrs. Pole's great grandfather, having died without leaving any heir to his marquisate, had been succeeded in the barony of O'Keefe by his kinsman, the grandfather of the statesman. "It is curious," he said dryly, when he reached the end of his narrative, "that the class whose special pride is to do nothing for themselves or their fellow-citizens, should be the only class who are privileged to have their histories written. But what I have just been telling you is really odd and interesting."

When they went into the drawing-room, Mrs. Pole was not there; and the Canon, after a variety of aimless and fidgety movements, was finally attracted towards the pastel portrait of the lady, which he had, as he said, so often studied before, and whose presence in that place he regarded with such serious indignation.

"Look, Dr. Clitheroe—look!" he exclaimed at last. "Here is what has been worrying me. That young lady we met in the garden is exactly like this picture—except, of course, that she was exceedingly tight-laced, that instead of a turban she wore one of those abominable fringes, and had, what this woman has not, that meretricious foreign look about her. Unfortunately how well one knows it!"

"Ladies' dresses," began the Doctor, "I'm afraid are lost upon me." But just at this moment Mrs. Pole showed herself in the doorway.

"He's coming," she exclaimed, with a trembling agitation in her voice, "Martin can hear the wheels. I have," she continued, "just been with poor Miss Drake, such a forlorn little object you never saw in your life. Dr. Clitheroe, I wish you would go up and try to comfort her. She always says 'the Word,' when you speak it, does her so much good. And listen—I'm sure you might safely tell her this—that my aunt, to my knowledge, has left her the large silver tea-urn, the old Worcester tea-set, and a house for her life at Lyncombe."

The Doctor mounted the stairs, bound on this work of mercy, with the busy action of a dormouse in a rotating cage. A moment later, a bell had been rung loudly, and Mrs. Pole and her son were exchanging salutations in the hall, with a quiet which had the semblance of indifference, though it had the semblance only. Taking his arm she led him into the dining-room, where supper was awaiting him; and the Canon forbore to follow them. He retired to the drawing-room instead, where he attentively contemplated the portrait, and consulted anew the history of the O'Keefe family in the peerage. With an unenlightened expression he at last subsided into a chair; and taking up a weekly review, and turning to an article of his own in it,

which bore the suggestive title of " The Debt
of Dives to Lazarus," he solaced his mind
with admiring a trenchant train of reasoning,
which would, if acted on, have deprived him
of his whole canonical income. He was
before long interrupted by the return of Dr.
Clitheroe, and almost on the heels of the
Doctor appeared Reginald Pole.

The new-comer had a face with clear-cut
features, and hair which just on the temples
was growing prematurely grey. In his look
there was a certain melancholy, combined
with activity and decision, and there was in
his whole bearing the self-possession and
gravity of a man unconsciously accustomed
either to command or receive attention. His
dress even, careless as it was, had a certain
air of distinction, which the best tailor
may fail to convey to his most fashionable
cloth.

Whatever sadness his features might have
when in repose, their expression changed,
when he spoke, into one of cordial welcome.
" My dear Canon," he said, " it is a real
pleasure to me to find you here; and Doctor,
for all your kindness I hardly know how to
thank you. I hope you have both of you
found some place to smoke in. My mother

is gone to bed. Will you have a cigar with me in the dining-room?"

Of the two clergyman the only smoker was the Canon; but they both moved as was suggested, the Canon, with a paternal gesture, pushing Pole by the arm. The Doctor condescended to a little whisky-and-water, and the trio were soon conversing with a pleasant but restrained animation.

"It is, Dr. Clitheroe," said Pole, "an odd coincidence that we both of us should be serving the State in much the same capacity. I represent the world, you represent the Church. Things ought to go well when the State is served by both."

"And I, Reginald," said the Canon, unwilling to be left out in the cold, "have had the honour—if it can be called such—of forming the mind of a Royal Highness in his teens. You and Dr. Clitheroe have been studying the condition of the people—the great problem. I have had to busy myself with the other end of the stick, a very different and less satisfactory operation."

"Ah, Canon," said Pole, laughing, "I know your republicanism from of old. But you have, at any rate, had the opportunity of serving the great cause by teaching a

prince directly his own miserable insignificance."

The Canon was a man, who, on his social
side, was extraordinarily thin-skinned. Gratified by deference, a slight stung him like a
mosquito; and worse than a slight was anything like a sarcasm. He might not have
suspected Pole of meaning either one or the
other, if there had not been a something in
his late pupil's whole manner, which, though
really nothing more than the natural result
of experience, seemed meant to announce
to him that their former positions were reversed; and now this flippant allusion to his
sacred democratic theories, coupled perhaps
with a glance at his social practice, made him
for a moment fret with surprise and anger.

"Princes, Reginald," he said, "are being
taught their miserable insignificance by a
greater teacher than either you or I." But
then with a strong effort he summoned his
temper back again, and, abruptly changing
the subject, said in an altered tone, "By the
way, there was a question about which I
wished to speak to you. Have you ever met,
when abroad, any of your O'Keefe relations?"

"Only the minister," said Pole. "I stayed
once for six weeks with him. There are any

number of others; but I never happened to meet them. I wish," he added pleasantly, "that I had. Though not very reputable, I heard they were extremely handsome, especially one of them, whose good looks were more than she could manage."

The Canon stared at Pole, full of perplexed horror, which, however, was gradually got the better of by curiosity. "There is a Countess O'Keefe," he said, "who is at Lyncombe now with a yacht; and this very afternoon she sent over to inquire after Miss Pole."

"There are," said Pole, "several O'Keefe families. One had a villa at Baden-Baden, and a mortuary chapel there, with a gold dome among the pine-woods. I knew of them by hearsay only. They were half Russian, or Polish."

"From what your mother tells me," cried the Canon, "these must be the very people. But what was that you said about one of the young ladies connected with them?"

"It was a story," said Pole, "that I heard only by accident; but it was so well known that there can be no harm in repeating it. The hero of it was half a Frenchman—well-born, very handsome, and rumoured to be immensely rich. The young lady, it appeared,

had promised to marry him; and scandal
said she forgot that she was not married
already. In cases like these, the usual story
is, that the man, when the time comes,
won't marry the woman. Here, however,
this usual story was reversed—and the
prudent young lady refused to marry the
man. Instead of being rich, he proved to be
very poor; and it was, so malice said, on
making this tragic discovery, that she broke
his heart by refusing to let him make an
honest woman of her. But all the O'Keefe
young ladies, they told me, were wild as
hawks, though this poor Countess Stephanie
is the only one that I remember even by
name. She has married, I think, since then,
a man who might be her father."

"Ah," exclaimed the Canon, "this one is
Countess Shimna. I see," he said, laughing,
"that you stare at me. I suppose I forgot to
tell you that the Countess O'Keefe who is at
Lyncombe, sent here a daughter as mes-
senger—a most striking young lady; and it
was about her I wished to ask you. The
moment I set eyes on her there was something in her that I thought peculiar; and I
see this evening"—the Canon here dropped
his voice, as if he were nearing a subject

almost too delicate to touch upon—"I see this evening that her face bears the most singular resemblance to that unfortunate portrait which has been allowed to hang here in the drawing-room."

"The portrait!" said Pole, reflectively. "Now, which portrait is it that you mean? Do you mean the beautiful Lady Thyrza Brancepeth, my great-uncle's heroine, and the heroine of Byron's poem?"

"I mean," said the Canon, "forgive me for speaking plainly—a shameful woman, no matter how beautiful. The portrait, Reginald, should not hang where it does. It is fit only for a certain species of house which a Christian man never enters, and of which Christian women should not know the existence. Come, let us learn to call things by their right names, and not speak of heroines when we mean—well, I won't say what."

"I confess," began Pole, with the faint dawn of a smile, "I always took the greatest possible interest"—he was going to say "in Lady Thyrza," but, with quick good-feeling, he checked himself, and continued in a changed tone, "an interest in strange likenesses. I confess I am curious to see this mysterious young relation of mine. As for

the likeness—well, Lady Thyrza Brancepeth
must have been some relation to her too.
She was originally Lady Thyrza O'Keefe."

"Indeed!" said the Canon, "indeed! She
is not in 'Burke.'"

"No," replied Pole. "For reasons with
which I think you will sympathize, her name
was intentionally taken out of that book of
life, the Peerage."

The Canon once again felt the mosquito's
sting. He fancied he detected a sarcasm
directed against himself in this allusion to
a volume of which he knew himself such a
frequent reader; nor was his inflammation
soothed by the few words which Pole said
next. They constituted a second sting,
malignant with a new virus.

"I really," Pole innocently continued,
"forget about all those relationships, if
indeed I ever knew. To-morrow, if you
like, we will speak about Lady Thyrza to
my mother."

"Speak to your mother," cried the Canon,
"about your uncle's adulterous mistress!
Reginald, pray be decent. My dear boy,
what can have come to you? You and I,
about these points, used to agree so well."

His old pupil repressed a slight gesture of

impatience, and said gently yet indifferently, "No doubt we agree still. I am glad, Dr. Clitheroe, that my aunt's end was painless."

The doctor looked up with a peaceful and serious smile. "Her last conscious act," he said, "was to receive the Sacrament."

"Yes," added the Canon, in loud and strenuous tones as he beat out the light of his cigar-end by dabbing it against a silver salver, "a death like hers is a really beautiful thing, and should give each one of us a robuster belief in life."

"My poor old aunt!" said Pole, as they all three rose. "She was very kind to me. Well, Canon, good night. What philosophers we should all of us be if we took our own deaths as easily as we do those of our friends!"

"Good night, Reginald," said the Canon, with magisterial coldness; and when he entered his bedroom he shut the door with a bang.

CHAPTER V.

IF the Canon went to bed indignant with his old pupil, and disappointed by him—brooding over the waste of his own bygone teachings, and still more over the complete evaporation of his own personal influence—Pole was conscious of a certain distress also. Having met the Canon again with a sense of cordial pleasure, he was conscious that almost at once he had jarred his feelings somehow; and he examined his memory in vain to discover exactly how: but he hoped that next day things would easily right themselves; and he rose next morning planning many civilities by which he hoped to conciliate his offended tutor.

The Canon's personality was at all events not far off from him. When he was just completing his toilet, his ears became conscious of a sound which he conceived to be caused by somebody grinding coffee. But

on entering the breakfast-parlour he found
that he had mistaken its nature, and that
it really proceeded from the Canon reading
family prayers. As he knelt down before
the nearest mahogany chair, and rested his
forehead on a surface of French polish, he
recognized the familiar phrases of the Right
Rev. Bishop Bloomfield, whose " Household
Devotions for each Day in the Week" had
been used at Glenlynn for more than half a
century; and he could not suppress a smile,
which was certainly not devotional, when he
heard the Canon, obviously much against the
grain, constrained to prefer the following
petition to Providence. "Make us humble
to our superiors, affable to our equals, kind
and condescending to the poor and needy."
It was a petition, however, of which the
Canon need have had no personal fear, for it
was plain when he rose from his knees that
in his case it had not been answered. He
was humble to nobody, and to Pole, instead
of being affable, he was distant.

Pole saw this with concern—a concern
that was all the greater because with each
little attention which he happened to pay
the Canon, the Canon's manner appeared to
become more frosty. Still this breakfast

was not an unpleasant meal; and for Pole there were many things in it which had a peculiar charm. The room, with its faded rep curtains, its faded sage-green walls, its old dumb waiters, and sideboard on whose glossy mahogany Georgian spoons and mustard-pots rested like swans on water, the dangling bell-pulls—one on each side of the chimney-piece—the turreted chimney-piece, Gothic, after the fashion of Strawberry Hill, the bright-coloured, large-patterned service of old Crown Derby, which shone on the table-cloth like roses placed on snow-drops—all these things touched him with many subtle associations. So, too, did Miss Drake, who had risen from dreams of her tea-urn, to find that family prayers still had power to comfort her, and who was so far in possession of her faculties as to be able, with her mittened hands, to unlock her tea-chest, and make tea as usual. Every object and incident reminded him of his earliest days, even the delicate, home-made wafer biscuits, and the butter-pats with the Pole crest on them: but everything now seemed charged with some gentle sense of loss; and once, looking at Miss Drake, who was munching a piece of toast, his eyes grew dim as he noticed how a dilatory tear traversed her cheek unperceived by her, and fell into her heap of salt.

As for Mrs. Pole, she had a pile of letters beside her, most of which, when she had read them, she passed over to her son. The Doctor mentioned that he had secured for himself a bed out of the house; and the Canon, without expressing any instant desire to move, explained how at any moment he could betake himself to Mr. Godolphin's. "I hope," said Mrs. Pole, "you will stay here, if we are able to keep you. I will talk with Reginald first, and see you a little later."

She and her son had a busy two hours together; and in the middle of a conference with the bailiff and an undertaker from Lyncombe, the air of the room was agitated by the entrance of Mr. Godolphin. He exhaled a fragrance of the Church, as if he had been a censer; but he brought with him also much practical sagacity, which, as he was not to have the privilege of burying Miss Pole himself, he consecrated to the task of suggesting how the mourners might be conveyed to her funeral. He undertook to engage all the flies in the neighbourhood;

he settled with the undertaker that there should be a special train to Lyncombe, which would bring, amongst other people, his Grace the Lord Lieutenant of the County; and many of the necessary arrangements he engaged to superintend himself. " I find that we can keep the Canon till the funeral, if he may come to you that night," said Mrs. Pole to Mr. Godolphin, as he rose to go. " At any moment," said Mr. Godolphin, " my house is yours." And with dignified rapidity he made his way to his carriage, proud to be bearing for his neighbours such congenial and important burdens. " Will you, Reginald," said Mrs. Pole, " go and tell the Canon. He'll be glad to have another couple of days to talk to you."

Pole, however, did not at once execute this commission. He went instead to the room where the dead was lying, and opened the door softly, with a useless, yet instinctive reverence. As he looked at the lifeless face he caught his breath and started, for what he saw was so strange, though it still remained so familiar. Death with the young is physically like mere unconsciousness; with the old it is sometimes a transfiguration. It was so in this case. Most of the wrinkles of a hundred years had disappeared; and there lay on the cheeks and lips a peace that was almost girlish, as if the waxen face had gone back to its own youth again, or the last sleep in its mercy had erased the writing of life.   Pole stood for some minutes at the foot of the four-post bed, on whose green curtains he had often gazed with awe in his childhood; and vague thoughts came to him, agitating the petals of memory, and blowing to him the scent of the days when his aunt had been a fairy godmother to him, and Glenlynn and its gardens formed a fairy-land filled with holidays.   The sound of the stable clock broke in on his meditations; and surprised of the lateness of the hour, he made his way downstairs, to look for the Canon, and convey to him Mrs. Pole's message.   His mind was softened and solemnized by this converse with the past and death. He felt a desire to be in charity with every human-being, as a fellow-communicant in the cup of a common destiny; and he was now more bent than ever on regaining an old friend's kindliness.

The Canon meanwhile had been in the library, reading with fierce satisfaction a newspaper paragraph in praise of one of his

own speeches. It was a speech which, a
few days back, he had delivered in St. James's
Hall, and in it he had contrasted what he
called "the two moral senses;" the moral
sense of the workers, and the moral sense of
the idle; "that is to say," he had explained,
"of the loafing or the propertied classes."
The Canon, in fact, had, during the past two
or three years, added to his democratic creed
certain new articles, which gave him much
agreeable notoriety in the columns of newspapers, and also, as he flattered himself,
much influence in the country. One of these
articles was that, next to inchastity, the
thing which required the most denunciation
was capital; and as he boasted that he had
never, since the day when he left Cambridge,
so much as looked into a book of political
economy, no one could have been better
qualified for attacking the latter evil. His
attacks on wealth in general had, indeed, of
late been so uncompromising, that some
sermons which he preached to a fashionable
congregation in Mayfair, conclusively proved
the fashionable luncheon to be stolen, at
which he was accustomed to refresh himself
after service. One of his great successes had
been a collection in behalf of a strike, when

a beautiful countess, who was more or less of a Magdalene, had handed the bag round with a grace that was almost irresistible. Some of his critics had been so unfair as to say that he looked on every strike as being, in its very nature, just. But there was one which occurred at a colliery in which he had himself some shares; and he considered that the knowledge and energy with which he denounced this, was a proof of the impartiality with which he supported others.

When Pole entered, he looked up from his paper sharply; but the message brought to him was, in many ways, so agreeable, and Pole's manner in giving it was at once so genial and deferent, that he suddenly thawed, and began to recover his conviction that his pupil was still under his healthy and commanding influence.

"My dear boy," he said, "your mother is, indeed, most hospitable, and I shall be truly glad of a few days' conversation with you. If you've nothing to do, what say you to this —shall we take a turn in the garden, and talk about old times?"

Pole assented, full of pleasant expectation, and the Canon, as they went, took his arm in an almost paternal fashion. He soon found, however, that the event was likely to disappoint him. The Canon found little pleasure in retrospection for its own sake; he was impatient of it, as a sentimental frivolity: and instead of dwelling on any personal memories of the past, he plunged into what he was delighted to call "the burning questions" of the present.

"There is one thing about you, Reginald," he said, "which does really rejoice me. I mean the fact that the work which has fallen to you to do is a work which has brought you face to face with realities—with the great problem of our time—that terrible spreading poverty which is a new social portent, and which I said in my speech last week may be called 'the shadow of capital.'"

"But, my dear Canon," began Pole, speaking as deferentially as he could, "is what you say a fact? Is poverty spreading? I have figures in my possession here—and besides, there are published Blue-books——"

The Canon, however, interrupted him. "Pooh!" he said, "a Blue-book will prove anything; and I don't care for figures—I trust to my own eyes. I have seen," he was about to say, "the poverty of the poor myself;" but his respect for veracity checked him, as he had long since settled with his conscience that his vocation with regard to the poor was to give them the benefit of his reasoning powers, rather than of his company. "My dear fellow," he said, "the fact is evident. Ask the people themselves. Not all the fudging of Blue-books will cheat them out of their own experiences."

The Canon was a man with whom to argue was to quarrel; so Pole, who was resolved to preserve not only his own temper, but his companion's, without retracting his own views, made no attempt to insist upon them, and for some time he listened submissively to the Canon's attacks on wealth, and his alternating doctrines that it should be possessed by everybody and by nobody. But at last he felt that he hardly could listen longer, and interrupting the Canon with the most careful and respectful gentleness, he said—

"I assure you that my interest in these problems is as deep as yours. But your labour and capital, after all, have to do only with the cup that contains life. The great question still for us is, what is the life that it contains?"

"Naturally," retorted the Canon; "and

who, do you suppose, denies that? Not I, at all events. To use your well-worn metaphor of the cup and the wine contained in it, who can insist more strongly than I myself do on the duty of each one of us to see that the wine is pure? You are aware, I suppose, of the particular Cause which I am now myself championing, and that is merely an incident in a larger moral movement."

"I was thinking of things," said Pole, with a slight sigh, "which are beyond the reach of movements, but which also belong to the moral world. I was thinking of the fidelity of a man to a woman, or of a father to his helpless child. I was thinking of those concentrated affections, which are the heart and the light of life, and of which your love for the community is merely the diffused reflection."

The Canon halted and looked Pole in the face. "And do you," he exclaimed, "really mean that the affections, as you call them, need no moral government—no control at the hands of Christian public opinion? What is corruption—what is vileness unutterable, except these same affections in their natural unchristian state?"

"Is there anything vile," said Pole, "in a mother's love for her children—in the eyes, the breast that move to the small hands calling for her, and to the lips on which language just begins to bud?"

"You are speaking now," retorted the Canon, "of nature, not of morals. Animals are good mothers till their young can walk and feed themselves. Where nature does well, let us leave her to her own devices. Our business, as Christians, is to fight against her when she does ill, and to arraign her before the presence of the God who is at once her creator and her judge."

"And yet," said Pole, "the conqueror of more than half of the Christian world was not the Judge and the Creator, but a mother and a little boy."

The Canon, who had been vaguely displeased by the whole turn the conversation had been taking, was irritated by this last observation almost beyond endurance. It irritated him partly as a respectful allusion to a Church which he tolerated with difficulty unless it happened to be represented by a cardinal; and it irritated him still more from the feeling with which the words were uttered. He disliked and distrusted all sentiment on principle, making only one exception in favour of righteous anger. "If that is so," he said dryly, "the Apostles might have spared themselves their trouble. The true Church is, according to your view, in the nursery."

"And if it were not there," replied Pole, unruffled by this sarcasm, "there would be little good in its being anywhere else. Look! some one is beckoning to us. That means luncheon. The two things," he added, absently, as if following out some train of thought, and as if his companion had ex-pressed no disagreement with him, "the two things that move me most are these—the child for whom we must do everything, and the dead for whom we can do nothing."

This last reflection might have been thought sufficiently harmless. There was nothing unchaste in it; nor was it an apology for capital: but, all the same, Pole felt, when he re-entered the house, that it had clenched his failure, in spite of his best efforts, to secure anything like a really cordial understanding between himself and one whose tempera-ment seemed to have risen in arms against his own.

CHAPTER VI.

AT luncheon the Canon was taciturn; but he ate with a vindictive vigour, as if converting the beggarly elements against their will to the service of Christian righteousness; and he afterwards set out by himself on what he said would be a ten-mile walk, treading heavily on the gravel as he started, like St. Michael trampling on the devil.

"I hope, Dr. Clitheroe," said Pole, when the two men were left sitting together in the dining-room, "I hope you will find your bedroom at the farm comfortable. When we have finished our coffee, shall we go and look at it? And if anything is wanting, we can send it down by this evening."

"I am sure," answered the Doctor, "I shall find everything I require; but I should like the walk. There are certain important reasons why I am anxious to have a little conversation with you."

The Doctor's manner expressed such kind and serious solicitude that Pole was set wondering as to what the conversation would refer to. The farm was about a mile off. It stood half-way up a valley which slanted down to the sea, and was reached from Glenlynn most quickly by a beautiful and wooded path, which ran along the cliff-side and hung over the waves and shingle. Along this they took their way, going slowly so as to enjoy the prospect.

"I suppose you know," began the Doctor, with a little nervousness, and a tremor of feeling in his voice, "I suppose you know the kindness—the exceeding kindness—which your aunt has shown me on very many occasions. Your mother, too——" The Doctor paused to clear his throat. "It is difficult to me now even to speak of all this kindness. What I wished to tell you is that in a small way—in a very small way—I have found myself able to repay it: and the way is one which nearly concerns yourself."

With each word of the Doctor's, Pole became more and more mystified.

"Your aunt," continued the Doctor, after a pause, "in many of her business matters was good enough to confide in my judgment;

and during her last illness she laid before me the entire state of her affairs. Of the main provisions in her will she made no secret; and you are probably yourself aware of them. She made no change in them at the last. The bulk of this property, with the house, is your mother's for her life; but a certain sum of money comes at once to you. The amount, roughly speaking, is about twenty thousand pounds, which used to bring your aunt about seven hundred and fifty pounds a year—a sum somewhat in excess of what she was accustomed to allow you."

"All this," said Pole, "coincides with what I have understood."

The Doctor stood still in the path, and with quiet eyes looked up at his friend. "You will," he said gently, "be far richer than you expected to be. The income you will receive will be much more like three thousand."

Pole could not help smiling, for the news had a pleasant sound. None the less, he stared at the Doctor incredulously. The Doctor was known to be a valuable public servant, but he was not reputed to possess much business ability; and the natural conclusion in this case was that he had somewhat muddled himself. He proceeded, however, like a person who knew quite well what he was talking about. "I see," he said, with his equally modulated intonation, "that you look surprised. I am glad to have been the means of bringing such a piece of good fortune in your way; and I know also that I was giving to your aunt a greater pleasure than to yourself; for you, I think, have always been rather careless of money."

"But, my dear Doctor," said Pole, "this sounds like a fairy-tale. By what process of alchemy can you have possibly worked this miracle?"

"That," replied the Doctor, "is precisely what I desired to explain. I have, as you know perhaps, served two Governments. My former chief, Sir Joseph Pilkington, to whom I owe my appointment, and who was pleased with what I did for him, was always of opinion that the stipends of myself and of one or two others were not commensurate with our work; and he was anxious to have them raised. But this he found impracticable. Subsequently he went to Australia, where he is at the present moment. You have heard of the Ridgehill and the Mount Mackinnon mines, the owners of which are now some of the richest persons at the Antipodes. Well,

Sir Joseph Pilkington was the moving spirit in this enterprise; but the capital required at starting, for various reasons, had to be raised in England. Firmly convinced of the enormous fortune that would be realized, Sir Joseph offered to myself and one or two of my colleagues the privilege of raising among ourselves or our friends a certain part of this capital, placing us in a position similar to that of holders of founders' shares. I invested myself every available penny I possess, and for the past five years I have been receiving twenty-five per cent. Well, owing to circumstances which I can explain by-and-by more fully, the opportunity has been offered me of investing a yet further sum, not to exceed fifty thousand pounds, either on my own behalf or that of persons nominated by me— investing it on terms not indeed the same, but yet approximately similar to those which I have mentioned. Interest will be guaranteed to the amount of fourteen per cent.; and when I show you the names of some of the guarantors, you will see that this now is no speculative business, but something as safe as Consols. Now, I was on the point, six months ago, of offering my only brother the opportunity of investing thirty thousand pounds, but he, poor fellow, died, and his son has turned out ill. I was, therefore, glad to offer the same opportunity to Miss Pole ; and for your sake she embraced it gladly and, I am sure, wisely. Of course, as I said, the sum is twenty thousand, not thirty. The remaining ten thousand—I tell you this in confidence—has been invested by Canon Bulman ; but he would not wish it to be spoken about."

" But are you sure," said Pole, "that the whole thing is sound? A safe fourteen per cent. really seems hardly credible. Would it not be better, before the money is actually sent, to talk the matter over with old Mr. Whilks, my lawyer?"

"Of course," said the Doctor, "the opportunity is exceptional ; but founders' shares constantly pay much more. As to your lawyer, I only wish we could have consulted him—for your own satisfaction, I mean. But there is one point which I must impress on you. It is absolutely necessary that this entire transaction should be kept private, as the favoured position which has been accorded to me might, were it known, excite— you can easily see how—any amount of angry feeling, not against myself, but against

Sir Joseph Pilkington. And this brings me to the point which I want to make quite clear to you. The money has been placed in my hands absolutely—it has already been sent, so we cannot recall it now—and thus, plain as the nature of the transaction will be, when you have heard its details, your reliance ultimately will have to be on my own integrity."

"Of course," said Pole, touched by the Doctor's manner, "I rely upon that implicitly. My only doubt has reference to the accuracy of your information."

"About that," said the Doctor, "you shall be satisfied very soon. But to return to yourself. I felt that, though I was sure you trusted me, I had no right in an important matter like the present, to force this trust upon you. I have, therefore, arranged that, should you not approve of this investment, you will be able to withdraw your principal at the end of the current year, or any subsequent time, at two months' notice. If you are wise, I think you will leave it where it is. In my bedroom at the farm I have documents which will explain all to you."

The bedroom, when they came to examine it, they found to be clean, but almost Spartan

in its simplicity. There was no carpet
except a strip by the dimity-curtained bed ;
the chairs were hard and cushionless ; and
on the dressing-table, ornamented with
tufted mats of crochet-work, was a looking-
glass, in which the Doctor's face assumed
the proportions of a spoon. The Doctor,
however, welcomed the accommodation as
delightful, and the room was littered already
with various little properties belonging to
him.

"See," he said with pride, "there is my
new type-writer, and my patent reading-
lamp, which I hook on to the blinds of the
railway carriage. That is the oil-stove in
which I can cook my breakfast—four and
sixpence it cost; and here is my latest
acquisition. See this lamp! I light it. It
makes my coffee; then, when my coffee is
made, whip!—up this catch goes, and out
goes my lamp."

The Doctor was a great collector of small
patent inventions, and had frequently testified
his gratitude to his hostesses at Glenlynn
by presents of ingenious button-hooks, tooth-
brushes, and new kinds of soap. Having
done the honours of his coffee-boiler, he
resumed his airs of business, and briskly

unlocking a black leather despatch-box, on which his address at Whitehall was printed in gold capitals, he produced a number of letters and other papers, and one after the other submitted them to Pole's inspection. The Doctor's method of explaining financial matters surprised him by its precision and its unostentatious lucidity. By the time the various documents had been put back in their places Pole's dominant feeling was a cordial sense of gratitude, which almost put out of his thoughts the actual advantage which had been conferred on him; and, though not an effusive man, he spoke his thanks with a sincerity which Dr. Clitheroe, by his expression, showed that he understood. They remained at the farm no longer than their business kept them; and when they began to walk back, the Doctor, as if considering himself thanked enough, delicately turned the conversation to general and indifferent topics.

Of the world, in the narrower sense of the word, the Doctor had seen nothing; but his professional experience had given him much knowledge of life, and his plans for his own future seemed to be modestly extending themselves. He talked of buying a yacht,

to assist him on his official journeys, and
asked Pole's advice as to the choice of a
house in London.

"How soft the wind is!" he said, raising
his tall, silk hat; "and how marvellous is
the beauty of these views! See, here is a
bench. Shall we sit down for a moment?"

They did so, and after a pause, emitting a
few "hems," he began again, not without a
certain shyness.

"There was one other little matter," he said,
"which I wanted to name to you; and I hope
—indeed, I think I may even say I am sure—
that you will take what I say in the spirit in
which it is said. I know from experience
that persons who come into an inheritance
frequently find themselves, for a not incon-
siderable period, poorer than they were
previously, instead of richer. In the case
of yourself, for instance, and of your mother,
the duties will be very heavy; and I was
thinking this morning that you would possibly—it is no uncommon case—find your
ordinary balance at your banker's hardly
equal to the calls on it. I have, therefore,
made bold to pay into your account a half-
year's dividend in advance, on the twenty
thousand I have invested for you; and this

will enable you, in case the necessity arises, to help your mother with any advances she may require. The cheque I have sent is for fourteen hundred pounds—a sum which I think will be sufficient to make things quite easy for you."

"My dear Doctor," exclaimed Pole, "you positively take my breath away! But, indeed, I cannot accept all this overwhelming kindness."

"So far as I am concerned," said the Doctor, "you may assure yourself that I feel no inconvenience. I only wish I did, because I should feel in that case that I was making some more adequate return for the kindness of your family to myself. Listen now. To convince you how easy it is for me to do this, and how little scruple you need feel in accepting so small a favour, let me tell you what my own income has been for the last five years. You must remember that this is in confidence."

"Certainly," Pole replied.

The Doctor proceeded in a soft, emphatic undertone, letting the syllables follow each other slowly. "Eleven thousand a-year," he said. "It is more, far more, than I know how to spend. I am, therefore, quite sure that you will not hurt me by refusing this trifling service which I have so much pleasure in doing you."

"My dear Dr. Clitheroe," answered Pole, speaking with more emphasis than was usual with him, " by refusing your kindness I feel I should be making you an ill return for it. You have made it easy for me to accept it, but difficult to thank you adequately."

"Very well, then," said the Doctor, in a gratified manner, "let us speak no more about it; though by-and-by there are a few more business details which I shall have to mention to you. It's late," he exclaimed, drawing out his watch. "Bless me, how late! But wait here another moment. Let us look at the view once more. How marvellously beautiful, how marvellously peaceful it is!"

Pole, though he had hitherto showed no signs of exhilaration, began at last to feel the influence of the Doctor's news, and the pleasure of unexpected wealth possessing him like an armed man. The scene itself contributed to this effect, as he sat for some minutes longer silent by the Doctor's side. Before them was glittering an oval of breezy sea, bordered in silver by the bark of a shining birch-tree. On the steep banks that embowered them, and descended below their feet, clumps of heather bulged between hazels and slender tree-trunks ; above miniature horizons of tall grass ferns raised their antlers, and gorse in the intricate twilight lifted its yellow stars.

CHAPTER VII

IF Canon Bulman's anxiety to stay on at Glenlynn was due to the wish he had expressed for the society of his former pupil, his wish was one which apparently he took small pains to gratify: for though, like a Christian and a gentleman, he was sufficiently civil to Pole, he never again sought him as a companion, or attempted a confidential conversation with him; but contented himself with aiming at him occasional darts of sarcasm, in the hope of shaming him back to his old allegiance. The Canon in fact was a person—and the type is by no means rare—who was not only offended by men who ignored his influence, but was also attracted to them by a sort of hostile fascination, till his self-esteem should be pacified by getting the better of them. He had, however, in prolonging his visit, other views of a less militant nature: and in these—as he learnt

at luncheon on the day before the funeral—
in these, at all events, he was not going to
be disappointed.

"Lord Wargrave," said Mr. Pole, speaking
with an air of half-distressed amusement,
"comes quite early this afternoon, and he
tells me he is determined to stop over to-
morrow. I can't think how we shall keep
him quiet, and I know he'll be discontented
with our cooking."

"He stayed 'ere twice," said Miss Drake,
"in Miss Pole's time, and he liked our four-
year-old mutton, which he said ate so
juicy."

"I'm glad of that," said Mrs. Pole. "And
then there's the old Madeira."

"He stayed with me once at Cambridge,"
said the Canon, "when I was a Fellow. I
had a famous cellar in those days, which
Lord Wargrave appreciated. He is a cousin
of yours, I think," the Canon added abruptly,
as if suddenly afraid he might have spoken
with too great freedom of so important a
man to a lady who had the importance of
being his relation.

"He's my husband's cousin," said Mrs.
Pole. "I am glad to find you know him.
You and he will amuse each other. He's

wonderful. He knows everybody. But this is not the worst. The Duke—the old Duke of Dulverton "—the eyes of the Canon glistened—"is also coming—not, however, till later. At first he meant to have gone straight to the church from Lyncombe. But I am sure that Lord Wargrave, who is staying with him, has made him alter his plans. He is such a cross old man—the Duke is, except when he's in a good temper. I suppose you would know I was Irish, because I said that." The Canon's radical soul swelled with reverence for a woman who could speak so naturally of a duke as a "cross old man"; and his just appreciation of merit, even in a great magnate, led him to observe how much he had heard of the Duke's talents. Then he silently meditated on what Mr. Godolphin had said—that the Duke also was somehow connected with his hostess's family. The world in general seemed to grow warm with sunshine: and however Reginald Pole might rub him the wrong way, he felt, as he surveyed the dining-room, that he was sitting in the right place.

Pole, Dr. Clitheroe, and the Canon were still sipping their coffee, and the Canon had taken a cigarette from a case of ruby-coloured

enamel—"a present," he observed inciden-
tally, "from Prince George of Finland—such
a good fellow—a right good honest fellow"—
when a boisterous peal came clanging from the
front-door bell, and Pole rose, exclaiming—

"There he is; that's Lord Wargrave!"

Lord Wargrave was a man who had
achieved European celebrity, not so much
for his own gifts, as his appreciation of the
gifts of others. He had never attempted
to distinguish himself either in literature,
science, or politics, or in any of the idler
pursuits which give brilliance to fashionable
life. He had, indeed, once been devoted to
the study of architecture, and had been
anxious, at his own expense, to add a chapel
to Westminster Abbey; but his only solid
achievement had been an Elizabethan house
for himself, which was so much too large for
his means that he lived usually with his
friends. He had never made a speech in the
House of Lords; he had published nothing
except some gossiping notes of his travels;
but he knew the motives, the aims, and the
histories of half the public men and beautiful
women in Europe far better than they knew
them themselves, and he certainly divulged
them with infinitely greater candour. He

was master of a fair property and a very presentable pedigree, and wherever this last happened to be defective, he had thoroughly repaired it by the aid of his vigorous imagination. All this produced in him a satisfactory dignity of deportment, which was, when he entered the dining-room, much admired by Canon Bulman. His hair, his whiskers, and his eyebrows were so many sandy-coloured bushes. His face, in repose, possessed a certain massive gravity, but took a hundred expressions when he spoke, like lights in disturbed water. Liking, as he did, men of most sorts and conditions, the clergy were far from forming any exception to his rule, and often, when laying down the law in the study of some country parsonage, he had, except for the want of a white tie, every appearance of being an admirable clergyman himself.

He greeted Canon Bulman, taking him by both hands. "This is," he exclaimed, "a quite unexpected pleasure." And when the Doctor was introduced to him, he said, "I was reading your last report yesterday. It's by far the most masterly thing of its kind I know."

He then seated himself, awaiting the

advent of his luncheon, and, looking round
the room with a slow, judicial scrutiny,
said—

"I tell everybody that this is the oldest
house in England. It is the only house
where the life is three generations old. If
your aunt, Reginald, had not been a rich
woman, I always maintain that she might
have made a large income, merely by showing herself to American tourists as the one
survivor of our old county aristocracy."
He was here interrupted by some dishes
being placed in front of him, and the voice of
the old butler, which murmured in his ear,
"What wine, my lord?"

"Madeira," said Lord Wargrave, with
sharp and unhesitating brevity, as he transferred two chops with their rosy juices to
his plate.

"I see," he began, pausing between his
mouthfuls, and addressing Canon Bulman,
"that you are still active as a captain of
the national conscience."

His utterance was grave, and Canon Bulman was much gratified by it; but under
the corners of Lord Wargrave's nervous
mouth there lurked, in company with a
few crumbs of potato, a certain ambushed

humour, which a keen observer might have
detected.

"You," said Canon Bulman, leaning forward with an ingratiating smile, "I am sure,
must be of our opinion, that it is impossible
for a man condemned publicly in the divorce
court to remain the leader of a great Parliamentary party, especially considering the
way the whole thing was done. Why, he
used to drive—I am told this for a fact—
down to Palace Yard with the partner of his
guilt, in a brougham."

"Did you ever meet the lady?" asked
Lord Wargrave, peering up at him.

The Canon frowned and bridled. "Never,"
he answered; "I am thankful to say, never."

Lord Wargrave looked at the ceiling, and
murmured in a reflective voice—

"A delightful woman, a most delightful
woman! The Archbishop of Monaghan
used to call on her every day. She wrote
that Report on Ireland which he sent to the
Pope—the whole of it."

The Canon knew not how to receive this
speech. Various expressions were in a state
of civil war on his face, and the eyes of
Lord Wargrave twinkled for just a moment.

When the latter had finished his luncheon,

his expression gradually altered. He leant over to Pole, and said in a resounding whisper—

"My dear Reginald, let me look at your poor aunt's body."

Lord Wargrave was an amateur of all kinds of emotion, and before he had left the dining-room he had pulled out a large silk handkerchief, so as to be ready for the tears which he meant presently to shed; and when, five minutes later, he emerged from the chamber of death, solemnly wiping the remaining moisture from his eyes, he felt as much warmed and exhilarated as if he had had another glass of Madeira.

The Canon, meanwhile, had recovered his equanimity, and sacrificed the craving of his muscles for a long walk to the unselfish pleasure of entertaining Lord Wargrave in the library, and helping him to examine its rows of curious and forgotten books.

"By the way," said the Canon at last, hastily closing a volume of French engravings which had held him for a minute or two in fascinated indignation, "do you happen to know and remember a certain pastel portrait here, which hangs in the next room?"

" I suppose you mean," said Lord Wargrave, " the portrait of the divine Thyrza. Beautiful, beautiful! That picture at Christie's would fetch at least a thousand guineas."

" I was not," said the Canon, dryly, " thinking of the merits of a picture whose presence in this house I consider to be in itself an indecency. What made me allude to it was a very curious fact." And he then described the appearance of the young lady in the garden, her singular resemblance to the portrait, and what he had gathered as to her family history. Lord Wargrave pricked up his ears. "And she was," the Canon continued, "not only like this woman, but she looked as if her career either had been, or would be similar. One of the family, Pole tells me, has gone desperately wrong already."

" Humph!" muttered Lord Wargrave into the space between his coat and waistcoat. " I've not the least doubt she's an extremely fascinating woman." Then, turning to the Canon, he said, "I should like to see her. I have in my own mind not the least doubt about the matter. Tristram Pole had a daughter by Lady Thyrza Brancepeth. Byron saw the girl, and mentions her in an unpublished letter. She was brought up in a convent, and married one of her mother's relations — a fire-eating count who fought under the first Napoleon. I've not the least doubt that this girl is her grand-daughter. With such a grandmother she has every right to be charming."

The Canon's face grew frigid. Out of the corner of his eye Lord Wargrave perceived this.

"Did you ever," he said, in a very serious voice, "hear these verses?

> 'Those myrtle-blooms of starriest birth
>   Were dim beside her breast of snow ;
> And now it sleeps beneath the earth
>   From which their sister blossoms blow.'

They come from the poem which Byron wrote on Lady Thyrza's death."

What would have happened to the Canon had the strain of the situation been prolonged, it is very difficult to say ; but at this juncture luckily the door opened, Lord Wargrave's eyes wandered, and he exclaimed, with extended hands—

"But, God bless my soul, who's this? Why, my dear old friend the Dean!" And

the next moment he was very nearly em-
bracing a stately gentleman in gaiters and
snowy necktie, whose face was fresh as a
foxhunter's, and who walked like an archbishop.

"I think, Canon," said Lord Wargrave,
"you must know Dean Osborne Pole. This,
my dear Dean, is the celebrated Canon
Bulman."

The Dean, though a high Tory and a hater
of clerical radicalism, greeted the Canon with
much fraternal condescension, and the Canon
returned the greeting with a courtly, yet
independent deference, which showed him
in his best light.

"I see, Wargrave," said the Dean, "you
have been having an afternoon among the
Muses. In this library there is, if I remember rightly, a remarkably fine collection of
early editions of the classics." And the
three gentlemen discussed books for an hour
or so, till Mrs. Pole entered, and was shortly
followed by tea.

"I hear," said Lord Wargrave by-and-by,
as he finished the last tea-cake, "that half
the county will be at the funeral; not only
men, but ladies; and perfectly right, too.
Such a death as this is like a Dissolution of

Parliament. The Duchess is coming, and old Lady Taplow with her. That," he murmured, patting the Dean's apron, "is one of the reasons that brings the Duke here." Then followed some story told in a whisper, which the Dean received with an expression of not very severe reproof.

"Ah, well," said the Dean, "dukes have their ducalities. Augusta," he continued, consulting a large gold repeater, "I will, if you will allow me, ask to be shown my room."

"Let me," said the Canon, with alacrity, "act as groom of the chambers." And he sprang to his feet like a boy; but just at this moment the door opened again, and a new arrival was announced—an old man, short and fragile, who stooped somewhat, and shuffled rather than walked. His clothes hung on him loosely; his grey hair was thin; and a pair of smoked glasses which eclipsed a good half of his face, made it hard to conjecture the meaning of the smile which hovered about his mouth. The moment he spoke, however, he gave some clue to the mystery. His hollow voice, his pronunciation, which bore the traces of some far-off dandyism; his elocution, which was emphasized by sententious pauses, and punctuated by soft and semi-malicious chuckles, all combined to render the smoked glasses transparent, and to betray the light beneath them of an alert but benevolent cynicism. This was the Duke of Dulverton, who had inherited from his father one of the most celebrated names in Europe—a name which he was wont to say with a caustic modesty, had been for himself an extinguisher rather than a pedestal. When Mrs. Pole went up to him he shook her by both hands; he greeted the Dean with benignity, and nodded at Lord Wargrave curtly; but most of his graciousness seemed to have been kept for Canon Bulman. The Canon was delighted, though the ducal words had been few; and he was by no means so anxious now, as he had been a few minutes previously, to quit the library and escort the Dean to his bed-room. The Dean, however, held him to his promise, and the two dignitaries departed. The Duke eyed the Canon's coat-tails as they disappeared through the doorway, and turning to Mrs. Pole, he said to her, "Is that your sniveller?" This was his private generic name for a clergyman; but though it certainly betrayed small reverence for the pulpit, there were few men in England from whom a larger number of clergymen had received greater and more thoughtful assistance than from himself.

"Oh, ho!" he said, when Mrs. Pole had set him right. "Canon Bulman, is it? You introduced him to my deaf ear. A shocking fellow, I know him—a shocking fellow! I thought he was too well-groomed for one of your hedge-parsons. To tell you the truth, I like the hedge-parson better."

In spite, however, of this opinion, when the party reassembled for dinner, the Duke's attention to the Canon was even more marked than before, though a certain spirit of mischief underlay his urbanity.

"I have listened," he said to the Canon, who sat next to him, "with great attention to your sermons in the Chapel Royal." The Canon bowed. "I invariably agreed," continued the Duke, "with the beginning of every one of your sentences." The Canon bowed again, with a puzzled and yet a gratified expression. "Would you like me to tell you why I didn't agree with the rest?"

"If you please," smiled the Canon, gravely.

"Because," said the Duke, laying his hand on the Canon's arm, "because I could not hear it." And he stopped abruptly, and glanced round the table. "Augusta," he continued presently, mouthing out the name in a tone which suggested the beginning of a speech in the House of Lords, "have you heard any more of that defaulting bailiff of Miss Pole's?"

"Nothing," said Mrs. Pole. "It is you, Duke, who should have heard, if anybody. It was your kindness which helped him to go off to the Colonies."

"Miss Pole," said the Duke, "had him on my recommendation, so I felt bound to look after him. I heard from him this morning. Do you know what he is now? Not one of you here will guess. He has just been elected a member of the New Zealand House of Lords. Dishonest men are dishonest only for one reason; that's because they are poor."

At these words the Canon actually started with delight.

"That," he exclaimed, "is the very doctrine which I am always preaching from the pulpit, and now and then from the platform; and that's why some people see fit to call me a radical. I'm glad to find that your grace is of one mind with me. Men are dishonest only when society makes them poor."

"Then in that case," said the Duke, facing round to the Canon, and speaking in a voice that had the air of being confidential, but which was nevertheless distinctly audible to every one, "in that case, if I were you, I wouldn't be so hard upon the rich."

Delighted as he was with this sudden thrust, he had no wish to discompose the Canon seriously; so, to cover the confusion he had caused, he addressed himself to Reginald Pole. "Reginald," he called out, "if I were a poor man you would probably find, when I am gone, that three or four of these silver candlesticks were missing. If you or Canon Bulman," he continued, "ever pay me a visit at Dulverton—if you will, Canon, I shall be very happy to see you—" at this the satisfaction in the Canon's face shone out again after a momentary eclipse— "I shouldn't advise you or any one else," said the Duke fiercely, "to make away with any of the spoons or forks *there*."

"Why so, your grace?" asked the Canon a little stiffly; and all stared with wonder at the Duke's sudden ferocity.

"Because they're not silver," said the

Duke, and closed his mouth with a snap. Having enjoyed for a moment the surprise which this explanation caused, "Most of my silver," he said, "is in the cellars of Childes' Bank. What I use at Dulverton is a copy in electro-plate. See, when you come, Canon, if you can tell the difference."

To the Canon's ear there was magic in the last words; and, on the whole, he enjoyed his dinner: but after Mrs. Pole had left the gentlemen to themselves, he began to be galled afresh in a place that was already aching. When Pole moved from his own end of the table and seated himself by the Duke, the Duke turned round, and edging as close to him as possible, became deaf to everybody else, and talked to him exclusively. He began questioning him about various European capitals, with most of which he himself had had formerly some acquaintance; and Pole's answers, which were more audible than the Duke's questions, betrayed an intimacy with the beauties of so many Courts, and with so many distinguished Continental families, that the Canon, who knew nothing of Europe but the peaks and table d'hôtes of Switzerland, felt—he could hardly tell why —as if he were intentionally shut out in the

cold.   This alone was a disagreeable thing
to bear ; but it was worse still when the
Duke, dropping his voice, made one or two
remarks which apparently related to ladies.
It was an axiom with the Canon, who had
the charity which believes all things, that
every whispered remark about a woman was
either cynical or indecent, or both ; but his
righteous anger was directed in the present
case not against his ducal neighbour for
making the remarks in question, but against
his former pupil for being the recipient of
them.   Lord Wargrave, too, was annoyed,
though for very different reasons.   He was
annoyed at being debarred, owing to the
presence of the three clergymen, from a
feast of philosophy and anecdote, in which
he would have gladiy joined ; but his sense
of propriety constrained him to make the
best of the situation, and as he could not
well take part in the gossip about Berlin and
Paris, he entertained the Dean, Canon
Bulman, and Dr. Clitheroe, by trenchant
accounts of the immorality of the country
priesthood in Spain.   The implied tribute to
the superior morals of Protestantism hallowed
this subject in the eyes even of the Canon ;
but before long the discussion of it was

interrupted by the voice of the Duke, whom the interest of some reminiscence had made unconscious of how loud he was speaking, and who was heard saying, in his most pointed and deliberate accents, " Her mother was my father's favourite mistress."

" Reginald," said the Dean, rising, " don't let me interrupt the Duke. I am going to have a little talk with your mother."

The events of the dinner-table had a double effect upon the Canon. They left him when he rose from his chair, and from contact with the Duke's elbow, elated with a delightful addition to his stock of social self-complacency; and they also left him more dissatisfied with Pole than ever. But Pole's offences against him were not even yet complete. The Canon's tenderest spot had thus far been only grazed by him. Before the evening was over he was destined to plunge a dagger into it. Some business about the funeral, which necessitated an interview with the bailiff, kept him for a quarter of an hour from following his guests into the drawing-room. When he did so, his mother and the Dean were talking together in low tones; Dr. Clitheroe was smiling silently; the Duke was apparently asleep;

and the principal sounds in the room were proceeding from the Canon and Lord Wargrave. The Canon, with the air of a complete man of the world, was discoursing to Lord Wargrave about society in the neighbourhood of Windsor; and as he saw Pole approaching, he unconsciously raised his voice. "No," he was saying, with reference to a well-known clerical liberateur — the author, amongst other things, of a manual of private prayers, which a crowned head had rendered popular by offering them up to Heaven—"no," the Canon was saying, "I don't think I exactly like him. Rather snobby, I fancy—rather fond of great people."

"I am never quite certain," said Pole, at whom the Canon had cast a lofty glance, "what it is that people mean by a snob."

"I mean," said the Canon, "and so I believe do most of us, a man who estimates others by who they are, not by what they are."

"I," replied Pole, "should venture to differ slightly from you. So far as the accidents of position have any effect on us at all, everybody's social judgments move roughly to the same tune; but the men whom you call snobs play each note a semitone wrong :

they distort the tune with false expression and emphasis, and very often," he added as an afterthought, " they pretend that they are not attempting to play the tune at all."

In his mind as he spoke there was no thought of wounding anybody. He was not even trying to put the Canon argumentatively in the wrong. But the Canon, for some reason, grew crimson to the roots of his hair. He bit his lip, and was stammering for some retort when a hollow voice sounded from the depths of an armchair. The speaker was the Duke, who, if he had slept at all, had certainly managed to sleep with one ear open.

" Canon," he said, " Mr. Pole is perfectly right. Mr. Pole had you there, I think. When the nation honoured my father by making him a duke, did they mean to give him something which others should not respect? No one," continued the Duke, in his best aphoristic manner—"no one deserves an honour who despises it; and no one despises it who receives it. Wait, Canon, till you're a bishop—as you are perfectly sure to be—and tell me what you think then."

So far as the Duke was concerned, Canon Bulman's feelings, outraged by the beginning of this speech, were charmed by the end of it into a state of renewed satisfaction; but it was only by all the efforts of mundane and Christian self-control combined, that he was able to be courteously civil in saying "Good night" to Pole, and in accepting from his hands a copy of the Lyncombe paper, which contained an account of the arrangements for Miss Pole's funeral on the morrow.

CHAPTER VIII.

A GOOD deal of arranging had indeed been necessary to facilitate the attendance of the large numbers that were expected. The church where the burial was to take place was some two hours' drive from Glenlynn, hidden in a deep valley: but a couple of miles on the Lyncombe side of it was a spot on the moor where several rough roads met, one having been a coach-road seventy years ago. Here stood a bald old inn, which had, since the days of coaches, been kept disconsolately alive by the patronage of a few stag-hunters; and at this spot the mourners from all quarters were to assemble. Here the hearse was to await them at half-past eleven; and here, in a room where travellers once breakfasted, they were subsequently to solace themselves with the funeral baked meats.

By the hour appointed the place wore a strange aspect. The lines of hedgeless road

were black with flies and carriages, the warm
gorse-scented wind blowing all August
through their windows. Some of the carriages were empty, but most had sable occu-
pants: and a number of figures also were
standing about the inn-door. Chief amongst
these was Mr. Pole, the head of the family,
six feet four in height, with a clean-shaved
commanding face; recalling a past age by
his voluminous white choker, and black,
swallow-tailed coat, buttoned across his
chest tightly. A little in the background
was the undertaker, taking charge of the
waving hat-bands, with which he had contracted to decorate the principal male
mourners, and, little as he thought it, to
give to the day's solemnities another touch
of an age that has almost vanished.

The last arrivals were the party from
Glenlynn. Their advent caused a considerable though subdued sensation; and the
carriages then began to be marshalled in
proper order. The family and their immediate friends meanwhile entered the inn;
where the hats of the favoured males were
indued with the insignia of sorrow. The
Duke alone was exempt, for the exceedingly
simple reason that he wore an old soft

wide-awake, on which no hat-band could
support itself; and the undertaker on
realizing this would hardly have recovered
from his bewilderment, if it had not been
for Lord Wargrave, who, with an impatient
grunt, tendered his own hat to receive the
orthodox treatment.

At length it appeared that the preliminaries
were settled: and the undertaker, backing
like a Lord Chamberlain, led his lugubrious
procession out to the line of carriages. In
front the plumes of the hearse slowly waved
and nodded, and wild bees and butterflies
passed and repassed between them. Presently a word was given; the dark plumes
moved onwards, and the carriages began to
follow like a train of crawling caterpillars.
The nature of the road in itself was enough
to make the progress slow; but in half an
hour it suddenly grew yet slower, this being
partly due to the steepness of a descending
hill, and partly to a fact which was announced
by the sight of some low-browed cottages,
and then by the throbbing note of a slowly-
tolling bell. Presently came cottages clustering more thickly; men—mostly old—were
walking along in black: the note of the bell
grew clearer: the carriages at last stopped.

There was hardly a cottage within fifteen miles of Glenlynn which Miss Pole's charity had not either cheered or pauperized: and a small, but sympathetic, crowd was assembled at the churchyard gate. The scene was singular. The church and the straggling village said to the stranger from every roof and window that progress never as yet had entered this secret hollow; indeed, the primitive aspect of everything almost appalled the mind, whilst captivating it. The church, for some reason lost in parochial history, was large and out of all proportion to the present number of the parishioners. It had been built in the fifteenth century; but its fine pointed windows showed, both in their glazing and their tracery, the repairing hand of the eighteenth; and its old-world air was most probably owing to its suggestions of that nearer past rather than of the more remote.

And now, from its opened door, what figure was this that was given forth to the light, and advanced between the mouldering tombstones—a figure whose old wig and dusty tumbled surplice made it seem as if both they and their wearer had been taken out of some forgotten cupboard? He shuffled in walking; his proportions were somewhat portly; and about his nostrils hung shadows suggesting snuff. His face, indeed, produced the impression of a man who was walking in his sleep; till suddenly his lips moved, and the following well-known words rose from them, distinctly audible, though thin in the open air: "I am the Resurrection and the Life, saith the Lord. He that believeth in Me, though he were dead, yet shall he live." And the palled coffin, with its bearers, had begun their movement towards the church.

The mourners followed—a long column of infantry—brushing the forlorn grasses that leaned over the grass-grown path, and defiling into the building through a porch, on whose whitewashed walls notices hung about ratepayers and licences for dogs and guns. Within the spectacle was one of which soon there will be no example left. The old square pews of the eighteenth century, some of them lined with moth-eaten green baize, filled the body of the church; and one of the aisles was dwarfed by a brown gallery. The clerk's desk, the clergyman's desk, and the pulpit, rose above one another, crowned with a huge sounding-board, on which stood a gilt angel blowing a dusty trumpet. The lion and the unicorn hung in a black frame, with the royal arms between them, over the middle of the chancel arch ; and a meagre altar, adorned with two velvet cushions, was flanked by a dingy board inscribed with the Lord's Prayer, and the table that begins with, "A man may not marry his grandmother."

Whilst the coffin, in the central passage, rested on its high trestles, the alien company gradually found places, stirring up, as they did so, odours of old prayer-books, musty hassocks, and many past congregations. Pole, who, on entering, had observed the gallery staircase, made his way alone to a solitude amongst the upper seats ; and filled with a swarm of thoughts, which he feared to betray to others, was able unnoticed to gaze on the scene below. Meanwhile, a sudden and unexpected sound had startled the ears of almost all those present. It was the sound of a fiddle, from which an old village musician, who supplied with his instrument the place of organ and organist, began to elicit the tune of a funereal hymn. To those, who, like Pole, knew the West of England well, and were aware that till up to the middle of the present century, a village

band of flutes, fiddles, and clarionets, continued in remoter places to supply the sole
church music, the wail of these notes was
as music coming out of a grave. To Pole
it rose pungent, like some bewitched incense,
fraught with everything that was dear and
past and impossible; and his own life, with
its secrets, whatever they were, enlarged
themselves, till his personal consciousness
was little more than a heart, beating and
palpitating with the hopes and losses of
generations. Then his attention strayed to
a mural tablet facing him, bracketed on coats
of arms, and surmounted by a willowy
female, whose straight Grecian profile
drooped over a marble urn. Straining his
sight somewhat he spelt out the inscription,
the very phrasing of which was sufficient to
fix its date. "In the adjacent vault, according to his own directions, are disposited the
mortal remains of Tristram Pole, Esquire,
eminent alike for the genius and the elegant
accomplishments which endeared him to
his Sovereign's son, and for his public
services to his country. He was for many
years Member of Parliament for this county,
and owner of Pole Park and its large
appendages. Reader, learn from hence the

vanity of all earthly possessions; but be also taught, by the signal example of one whose charitable hand was ever open to the poor, to cultivate that special virtue which, more than any other, recommends man to his Creator and covers a multitude of sins."

But he had hardly come to the end when he realized that the fiddle had ceased and a single voice was snuffling through the musty silence. "Behold, Thou hast made my days as it were a span long; verily every man living is altogether vanity." Then the voice sank to a long monotonous murmur, interrupted only by the lilt of two doxologies, to the shame-faced singing of which the assembly was stimulated by the fiddle.

Pole had been listening in a fit of vague abstraction, moved by his surroundings he hardly knew how or why: and at length he leant forward, half kneeling, with his face buried in his hands. His mental condition, in common with that of so many, was such that the service could not possibly mean to him what it has meant to those who have listened to it for so many centuries. Its formal meaning for him was the form of a myth or fable; but there was something in it—a something not to be crystallized into words—which sank deep into his being and touched those roots of life from which all religion springs—all religion that is more than a lost chapter of chemistry. With a painful tenderness his thoughts began to fix themselves on two other lives connected with or dependent on his own, and he mentally began to offer up his own happiness for the sake of theirs, placing it, as it were, upon an altar, and offering it for his own sins also; until, as he knelt in spirit, it seemed to him as if a fire from heaven streamed through the cold and darkness, and consumed the sacrifice and accepted it.

But such visions are transient whatever their meaning or their effects may be; and Pole was roused from his by a rise in the clergyman's voice, which brought the following syllables poignant and piercing to his ear —" It is sown in corruption; it is raised in incorruption "—and reminded him, among other things, of how far the service had proceeded. At the same moment he distinguished what before had escaped his notice—a black wound gaping in the pavement of the aisle opposite; and he then recollected that the interment would be inside the church.

The open vault, however, was not all that
he saw. On turning his head slightly, he
perceived with some surprise, that he was
not, as he had thought he was, alone in
the gallery any longer. In the pew next to
his own were two female figures. But he
probably would not have bestowed a second
glance on them if he had not been roused by
a breath of some incongruous perfume. He
looked ; and a slim hand, delicately gloved in
black, caught his attention resting on a mil-
dewed prayer-book. Then he realized the
crisp curves of a figure which a dark jacket
emphasized with fastidious outlines ; and,
on raising his eyes, a pair of eyes met his
which held his own in one long astonished
scrutiny. They were the eyes of the pastel
portrait ; only far down in their depth,
shining between their long lashes, there
was, mixed with feeling, a faint sparkle of
espièglerie. Of what he did he was altogether unconscious ; but he knew he must
have made some sort of movement towards
her, for, shaking her head slowly with a
gentle smile of deprecation, she just raised
for a moment one reproving finger. But at
this juncture a stir took place below. The
coffin was being lifted, and numbers were

making their way towards the vault. Pole, with a hasty gesture, prepared to do so likewise; but in the act of going he hesitated, and, leaning towards the fair stranger, he said in a grave undertone, "Would you care to come down too? I know you. I am Reginald Pole; and you are Countess Shimna O'Keefe." She was like a woman who is encountered in a dream, and who is surprised at nothing. She replied in a tone that was even lower than his own, "I would rather remain here. Go—you must go alone."

A moment later he was standing by the dark aperture. The sentences of the Burial Service were being read at intervals like minute guns, and the coffin was being lowered slowly. In the gloom underneath were lights, and by means of a dirty ladder the Squire, Lord Wargrave, and several others descended. Pole followed them. The cold walls of the vault lisped with unwonted echoes as men shuffled and pushed each other, settling the coffin in its place. At last somebody touched his sleeve respectfully, and put into his hand a trowel filled with something. He saw it was earth. He threw a little on the coffin lid, and the words, "Ashes to ashes," were heard in the air above. As he performed this office the words " Margaret Pole " gleamed up at him in silver as yet untarnished ; and at the same moment the candle-light revealed another inscription, which now was quite close to this one, and which he stooped down to examine. What he saw was a text some- what abbreviated from the original : " The mother may forget her sucking child, yet will I not forget thee." This struck him as suffi- ciently, though not signally appropriate, until through the thick dust he made out a few words more—" Tristram Pole," with the date of his birth and death ; and then it dawned on him that the dead man might have chosen the text himself, with a meaning somewhat different from that which his orthodox relations must have attributed to it.

As he climbed the ladder again the elocu- tion of the officiating clergyman struck him as having grown unaccountably more im- pressive and sonorous. It imparted the vibrations of a bell to the overwhelming sentence that was being uttered. " I heard a voice from heaven, saying unto me, Write, From henceforth blessed are the dead which die in the Lord : even so saith the Spirit ; for they rest from their labours." Pole stared at the speaker, and instead of the old incumbent who had, as he heard subsequently, been seized with a fit of hoarseness, and had retired to suck lozenges in the vestry, his eye rested on the form of the Rev. Sunderland Godolphin, arrayed, it is true, in a surplice much too short for him, but, in spite of this trivial detail, more imposing than ever, and at last doing justice to Christianity, to his auditors, and to himself, by showing how the Church of England could bury her children when she chose. For him, at all events, the solemnities had not been performed in vain.

The concluding prayer at the grave had not come to an end before Pole had escaped from the crowd, and stolen back to the gallery; but he found it entirely empty. He had scanned the figures below, but failed to distinguish what he was seeking. He descended the stairs hastily, and at the bottom was an old bell-ringer, who asked him "if so be he was looking for two ladies;" and who, on being answered "Yes," replied, with a senile grin, "That the ladies had left in a carriage ten minutes ago."

A moment or two later everybody was once more in the sunlight. The sky glowed with blueness, the air smelt of grass and

summer, and faces hitherto rigid brightened
into discreet smiles. By the time the inn
was reached again the smiles had rippled
into laughter. Clergymen, lawyers, doctors,
and tenants on the Pole estate exchanged
greetings with the great county magnates;
and Lord Wargrave, who alone stuck to his
waving hat-band, looked about him fussily,
as if surprised at not being recognized.
Canon Bulman, by an unconscious instinct,
hovered in the Duke's neighbourbood, and
found himself sitting next him when the
party settled down to their refreshments.
Old Lady Taplow, however, who was on
the Duke's further side, took possession of
the ducal ear, and the Canon could only
listen.

"It was very touching and picturesque,"
she began in her gruff, masculine voice.
"I am glad that you made me come. By
the way, Duke, I ought to thank you for the
cheque you gave me for my bazaar. It was
kind of you. You're a good man, Duke."

"And you," said the Duke, "are a good
woman—so far as I know, that is to say—so
far as I know." The Canon swelled with
anger at the tone of this flippant innuendo,
and, cultivating the emotion, felt proudly

that he was no sycophant. He turned away, and found that his other neighbour was Pole.

"Somebody," he said sarcastically, as he glanced round the table, "will be proposing the bride's health soon. People are far more cheerful here than at most wedding breakfasts."

"Well," replied Pole, "is not that as it should be? A death is the ending of sorrow, and a wedding is generally the beginning of it."

CHAPTER IX.

CANON BULMAN, when the funeral feast was over, instead of returning to Glenlynn, was claimed by Mr. Godolphin, and his place was to be taken by the old family lawyer. The day being Saturday, the rest of Mrs. Pole's visitors were to stay till Monday; and Mr. Godolphin had been rendered happy by her promise to bring them all to his Sunday morning's service. As they were standing by the carriages and settling how to seat themselves, Dr. Clitheroe, with a little nervousness of manner, touched Pole's arm, and said to him in a confidential whisper, "Do you think you would care to walk the last two miles of the way? We have had no exercise, and I should be glad of a few words with you."

"Certainly," Pole replied. "Let us get in here then with Miss Drake." And by-and-by, when the swelling downs were reached which hid Glenlynn between their bare shoulders and the sea, he and the Doctor descended, leaving Miss Drake alone —a little abstracted bundle of silence, and crape, and tears.

"I have had," said the Doctor, "during the last few days no opportunity of explaining a small matter to you. Your mother understands it. She, naturally, has my entire confidence; but the whole arrangement—I am sure you will not forget this—must rest a secret between our three selves. Your lawyer, Mr. Whilks—I presume he is coming here for the purpose—will presently take possession of your aunt's will, and explain its provisions to yourself and others. Now I want to tell you beforehand that in the will itself you will find no money left to you till after your mother's death. The reason, of course, is that your twenty thousand pounds had to be realized during Miss Pole's lifetime, and, as I have explained already, placed in my hands to deal with. Well," the Doctor proceeded, "the difficulty in our way was this: how to ensure your succession to the sum in question, and yet to keep the transaction secret, as I was bound to keep it. Your aunt wished to confide entirely in my own honour, and to leave in my custody all the papers connected with it. That proposal, however, I could not entertain for a moment. She and I, therefore, hit upon this device. A document, signed by me and accompanied by a letter from herself, was placed in a sealed packet. It was directed to you, and deposited with other valuables in a safe, and this packet is expressly left to you in the will, described ' as containing certain papers and memoranda, explanatory of my conduct with regard to the said Reginald Pole, which packet I desire that he open and read in private.' If you will look here," said the Doctor, pulling out a large pocket-book, " I can show you a duplicate of a formal document, in which the receipt of the money is acknowledged by me, and the terms on which I received it are stated."

The Doctor produced a large sheet of fools-cap paper, which bore the stamp of the Government Office to which he belonged, and on which the following form was engrossed in a clerk-like hand, the names and dates being faintly written in pencil: " Received for investment by me, the under-signed, from Margaret Pole, of Glenlynn, spinster, on behalf of her great-nephew, Reginald Osborne Pole, Esq., the sum of twenty thousand pounds. I undertake to pay interest quarterly on the above sum, at the rate of fourteen per cent. per annum, the same to be paid to the aforesaid Margaret Pole during her lifetime, and after her death to the aforesaid Reginald Pole, his heirs, or his assignees. This arrangement is to hold good for eleven years and five months from the present date, at the end of which period I reserve the right of repaying the principal. Further, after five months from the present date, I engage to repay the principal, should this be desired, at any time that may be named, two months' notice having been given me. In the event of my death, the above arrangements will be carried out for me by my colleague, Edward Stuart Michell, Esq., Inspector of Technical Schools for England, who will represent me in this transaction."

Pole looked the paper through, and gave it back to the Doctor, merely observing, "I am glad that my mother understands. She would else have wondered at my having been left nothing. As it is, I suppose old Whilks, who knew something of my aunt's affairs, will be puzzled at the personal property being less than he probably imagined it."

"I don't think," replied the Doctor, "we need have any fear of that. This last will, like the former one, was drawn up by Mr. Whilks himself, and your good aunt explained to him that she had spent a portion of her capital. The statement was strictly true, for, as you will see from the paper I have shown you, the twenty thousands pounds were virtually transferred to you during her lifetime. No," continued the Doctor, rubbing his hands gently, "since you and your mother understand the transaction, there is nothing in the will which will elicit comment from anybody." The Doctor's prediction in this respect proved substantially, though not literally, true; for when the contents of the will came to be known in detail, so many were the legacies left to old servants, and so far beyond her humble hopes was the provision made for Miss Drake, that the sense of Miss. Pole's loss, which had thus far been a grey cloud, was already illuminated by the spreading light of resignation.

By the following morning the progress in Christian cheerfulness was remarkable, when

Mrs. Pole, in a large open waggonette, conveyed her party to Mr. Godolphin's church.
Mr. Godolphin, too, when he saw through
the vestry window the heads of the Pole
horses tossing themselves at his churchyard
gate, felt his heart agreeing with the text
of the sermon he was about to preach, and
acknowledging that death had been partially
swallowed up in victory. His own chancel,
with its altar and surpliced choir, its brass
lectern, its crosses, and brilliant scrolls,
seemed by contrast with the one he had
visited yesterday, more perfect than ever to
him in its modest catholic beauty. It touched
him afresh by the effect which he felt it
would have upon the strangers; and when
his organ, from its rows of spruce blue pipes,
began to flute forth a very creditable volun-
tary, he silently thanked Heaven at being
thus permitted to offer to it such music as
would not ascend to it from any other village
in the county. But the climax was reached
when his choir, being duly robed, poured
through the vestry door and took their appointed places. Then, slow and stately,
came Mr. Godolphin after them, the sleeves
of his surplice swelling with some wind of
the spirit. The organ reverently hushed

itself, and "Dearly beloved brethren" prolonged, and, indeed, outrivalled, the music
of its silenced diapason. Mr. Godolphin
proceeded with his ministrations, as if conscious that the service was not prayer only,
but a lesson in prayer; and when he reached
the passage, which always had been his
favourite, "High and mighty, King of kings,
Lord of lords," he produced the impression, as Lord Wargrave observed subsequently, of being "himself the great Sublime
he drew." Nor was his sermon unworthy
of what preceded it. It was really in excellent taste, and instinct with unfeigned
emotion; and no dispassionate student of
human nature could have avoided feeling, in
spite of his guileless vanity, an affectionate
respect for him, as his periods hung and
echoed amongst the rafters.

When all was over the party from Glenlynn
waited to speak to him in the churchyard,
where they were first met by his wife—a
lady whose native kindness expressed itself
in a county accent. Mrs. Godolphin had a
pronounced taste for colour; and she usually
celebrated Sunday with a display of glittering ribbons, which made her look like a
yacht on the morning of some grand regatta.

But now she was all in black, and her
ribbons hung their heads, as she held Mrs.
Pole's hand, and, glancing shyly at the
others, said that " Dear Sunderland " would
be there in another moment. In another
moment he came, glossy in long black cloth,
and standing bareheaded, as if, whilst he
was on consecrated ground, he was, in some
special and spiritual sense, indoors, he bowed
majestically on being introduced to the two
peers ; and turning to the Dean, told, though
he hardly knew it, one of the few untruths
of his life. " Had I been earlier aware," he
said, "that there was any chance of your
being here, I should have asked you if you
would have preached this morning. Canon
Bulman," he continued, "has taken a service
at Lyncombe. I trust, Mrs. Pole, that you
—all of you—are going to stay for luncheon.
We counted on your doing so—Mrs. Godolphin and myself." This invitation was entirely unexpected ; and Mrs. Pole was on the
point of refusing it, when a vision rose before
her of a table laid for ten, covered with pies
and chickens, crackers, and coloured jellies,
and of the sadness of two human beings, if
they alone sat down at it. After a little
hesitation, therefore, the proffered hospitality

was accepted, and the whole party bent their steps towards the Vicarage.

Mr. Godolphin turned inclusively towards the Dean, Lord Wargrave, and the Duke. "I hope," he said, "you were pleased with our little service."

"Very much so," said the Duke. "I shall take your chancel for a model, whenever I have the courage——" He paused.

"The courage to do what, Duke?" said the Dean.

"The courage to deprive the Duchess of our old family pew."

"I don't know, Dean," said Mr. Godolphin, elated by this praise, and betraying in his voice a gentle amused triumph, "if you have seen the letters about me in the last week's 'Western Times?' There I am, gibbeted—as near Rome as possible." And as he spoke he shone with all the delights of martyrdom.

It was shortly after this that Lord Wargrave, nudging the Duke with his elbow—an attention which the Duke hated—muttered his observation about Mr. Godolphin and "the great Sublime." The Duke, however, entirely ignoring the witticism, replied sententiously—

"I thought the passage remarkably well read. I'll tell you what," he continued, with a little malicious laugh. "You, Wargrave, have seen a good deal of the world. Did you ever observe this, that bad men may have many follies, but only good men have foibles? Mr. Godolphin is a thoroughly good man. If I were the Deity, I should listen to him with a great deal of pleasure; and if he were a poor man I should give him my best living."

Lord Wargrave felt the dig; he received digs very often; but nothing wounded him, and he was rarely even perturbed. He was not so now; and when he seated himself in the Vicarage dining-room, and perceived the amplitude of the hospitable repast before him, his friendship for Mr. Godolphin almost surpassed the Duke's. After luncheon, Mr. Godolphin happened to mention that he was sending his carriage to bring back Canon Bulman. Lord Wargrave, on hearing this, went up to Pole confidentially and said to him—

"Would you be disposed to come into Lyncombe with me? We can get a lift, and return to Glenlynn in a fly. It occurred to me I might as well take the opportunity

of going and calling on my old friend
Countess O'Keefe."

"You know her then, do you?" exclaimed
Pole, with surprise and interest.

"I've known half the family," said Lord
Wargrave, "at one time and another; and
I've not a doubt when she sees my card,
she'll remember me. Besides, she's your
own relation. It is only proper you should
call."

Pole, however, required no pressing. Mr.
Godolphin was delighted that the services of
his carriage were appreciated, and the two
gentlemen drove off in it triumphantly.
When they reached Lyncombe, and descended the precipitous hill, which zigzags
down to the port between villas and hanging
gardens, the very first object that glittered at
them and caught their attention was a smart-
looking steam schooner lying near the
primitive pier, and lighting up all the prospect with its awnings and flashing hand-
rails.

"I thought," said Lord Wargrave to Pole,
when the carriage had set them down—and
he took his arm and spoke in a confidential
mumble--"I thought it as well not to
mention this visit of ours to your mother.

She was not particularly warm in her wishes to meet these ladies; but when we have seen what they are like, I have no doubt we shall be able to tell her they're everything that is correct, well-bred, and delightful."

Pole was somewhat amazed at Lord Wargrave's speculative condition with regard to a person he had spoken of as an old friend; but he had not fully realized that this remarkable man, who had thrown the net of his acquaintanceship over most of the civilized world, assumed that he knew everybody, till events proved the contrary, and that he would then make a new friendship in discovering it was not an old one.

"We must get a boat," said Lord Wargrave, as with a somewhat imperious gesture he tried to attract the attention of an old, somnolent fisherman. But Pole interrupted him and pointed to a couple of figures, lounging at a little distance, with caps scarlet as poppies, and spruce blue jerseys, which were seen, on a nearer view, to carry in white letters the outlandish word "Moshiska." Lord Wargrave, always happy to exhibit his accomplishments as a linguist, addressed the men in Italian and then in German, as if taking it for granted that they were natives

of Trieste or Fiume. They answered, however, in the tongue of the Isle of Wight.
"The Countess," they said, "was on board;"
and in a minute or two more he and Pole
found themselves at the yacht's side. Lord
Wargrave's hand was in his pocket, about
to produce his card-case, when a fit of shyness, rare as an angel's visit, urged him to
shift the burden of self-introduction to his
companion. "Send up your card," he said,
"and I will write my name on it." The
card was sent, and with a very flattering
promptitude the visitors were invited to
ascend. They found themselves in a world
of deck-houses, deck-chairs, and plump red
cushions littered with Parisian novels.
Amongst some of the cushions in the stern,
there was, as they followed their conductor,
a disturbance of blue serge and bright
cherry-coloured bows; and a tall lady had
risen and was coming forward to meet
them. Her figure was full but had not lost
its outlines; an infantine straw hat, with
"Moshiska" written on its ribbon, surmounted rippling hair which recalled the
yellow of a mimosa blossom; and her face,
though it showed the lines and contours of
sixty, was radiant—thanks to her powder

puff—with the dust, not of age, but of youth.
Both her hands were extended in gracious
welcome, to Pole first, and to Lord Wargrave
after him.   Her voice was charming; she
had a faint foreign accent, which produced
the impression that she would have been
very sorry to lose it; and her manner had
just that one unnecessary degree of *empressement,* which betrays in a woman that civility
has an added value for her, because, for
some excellent reason, she no longer always
receives it. " I was so distressed," she said,
ringing her r's, "to hear, Mr. Pole, of your
poor old aunt's death. My daughter and her
maid went to witness the funeral. And your
mother—she wrote me such a pretty, nice,
kind note. I knew her as a girl. She is well
now? Yes?   That's right, then.   Lord
Wargrave, do be seated. We have met, you
say. Was it at Baden?"

" That's the worst," said Lord Wargrave,
who was in the depths of a chair by this
time—" that's the worst of meeting a charming woman. The fact remains so vivid it
makes one forget the circumstances."

" You were staying then with the Grand
Duke, were you not?" said the Countess,
helping him out. "We had not time, I

think, for much conversation together. It
was the year when that silly little Ladislaus
—a perfect boy he was, a baby—you remember him with his great *boutonnière* — was
said by everybody to be *au mieux* with the
Grand Duchess."

Lord Wargrave remembered. At once he
was on solid ground. "The united ages,"
he said, "of the Grand Duchess's lovers,
would make a smaller total than those of
any other women in Europe." He and the
Countess now perfectly understood one
another; and even if, as seemed possible,
they had never so much as spoken previously,
they were soon conversing as though they
had been lifelong friends. Nor was Pole by
any means left out in the cold. She said to
him, "Will you order tea for me? You see I
treat you like a relation. And be a good
man, do; and fetch me my cigarette case.
It is lying there by a book—oh, such a book,
mon Dieu! It is called ' *Les Lèvres de Violette.*'
My cousin Bobrovski sent it me."

"Is that the prince—the traveller?" said
Lord Wargrave. "Why, God bless my soul,
I met him by the Dead Sea, when he was
straining his eyes to distinguish the sub-
merged public buildings of Gomorrah. I

saved his life, I remember, by giving him a package of tinned pigs' trotters."

"He's coming here soon," said the Countess, with the faintest air of embarrassment. "The yacht is his. He is a dear fellow, and he lent it me. I was," she went on, as if hurrying over delicate ground, "told that the sea air would be good for my daughter's health; and this place was particularly recommended to us. She's been nervous lately, and there's been a little something wrong with the chest; and she would, for many reasons, like a place that was quiet. We've seen a little thatched cottage with which we are all charmed; and when some of our servants—our old servants —can arrive, we shall most likely leave her here for a couple of months."

"And where is Countess Shimna now?" asked Pole, who had been patient hitherto only because each moment he expected the young lady's appearance.

"She's gone with her maid to church," said the Countess, poising a cigarette between two fingers laden with pearls and diamonds. "She sets you a lesson. You should both be hearing a sermon, instead of sitting and talking nonsense here with me. You laugh! I should have heard mass myself at eight o'clock this morning, but the carriage did not come, and I am forbidden to walk up-hill."

"Well," said Lord Wargrave, "here are two father confessors, eager to hear your sins, and to tell you in absolution that they are far more charming than the virtues of other people."

"Ah," said the Countess, with a gay ripple of laughter, "that is good now! I'm afraid they'd be a long catalogue."

Pole meanwhile was beginning to think wearily that, since Countess Shimna was away, the visit was a waste of time; so, consulting his watch, he said, "If we wish to be back for dinner, I fear we must say good-bye, and ask to be put ashore. My mother, Countess, is hoping so much to see you; but if business prevents her this week from driving over to Lyncombe, perhaps you and Countess Shimna will come one day to us at Glenlynn."

"Your dear mother!" exclaimed the Countess, evidently pleased at this overture, but once again betraying some slight em-barrassment. "As for me, I am not strong enough for visiting. I must wait, too, and see what my cousin Bobrovski has settled for me. But as for Shimna—she, I am sure, will be delighted to see your mother. Write —do write—and tell her a day for coming."

Pole was by this time standing, ready to say "good-bye"; but Lord Wargrave, who seemed each moment to be sinking deeper in a quicksand of cushions, was far from showing the smallest inclination to move. "My dear fellow," he said, "you are happily young and active. Will you order the carriage for us? and when I see it on the pier, I will join you."

Pole readily assented, feeling now that the visit had been a success. Though his mind, since his meeting with Countess Shimna, had been occupied with other things, the memory of her at odd moments had been frequently shining through them at him, and he was conscious of a curiosity with regard to her which surprised him, and which he tried to stifle. At this moment, however, it was possessing him unreproved, and his thoughts were busy with her appearance in the old church, when the boat that was taking him back bumped against the harbour steps. As he landed he heard that the men said something; but he did not realize what, till, on reaching the topmost step, he saw that the

subject of his thoughts was herself standing
before him.   Again for a moment, just as
in the gallery of the church, their eyes
exchanged an unflinching and full regard.
Then her lips smiled, like an opening rose-
bud.   She put her hand out to him.   He
took it, and held it lingeringly.

"I have been," he said, "to call upon your
mother.   Lord Wargrave is with her still.
We are just starting for Glenlynn.   I am
going to get a carriage.   My mother means
to write, and ask you to come and see us."
The sentences came with a sort of unconscious shyness.   Something of shyness
showed itself in her also, for she several
times drew breath as if meaning to begin a
sentence.   She was silent, however, until
he came to an end, and then she said simply
and almost tremulously—

"I should like that.   Good-bye; I must go
now."   She again gave her hand to him, and,
withdrawing it with the soft slowness of a
wave withdrawing itself from the sand, she
went down to the boat, and the water was
soon between them.   He made no attempt to
keep her.   He did not turn to watch her
even.   On the contrary, he walked sharply
away, anxious to make sure of the memory

before it had time to alter—the memory of that butterfly of a moment, before a detaining touch had been able to brush from its wings one of their fragile colours.

"The mother," said Lord Wargrave, as they drove home together, "is a dear, delightful woman. Her cousin Bobrovski is evidently of the same opinion. Perhaps we can hardly expect your own mother to agree with him. But as for the daughter—well," he grunted, as if fumbling about for a phrase adequate to his meaning, "she's the sort of woman to make any man under fifty mad."

That evening on the terrace at Glenlynn he again returned to the subject. He and Pole had, both of them, after dinner been tempted out of doors by the moonlight and the breath of the verbena beds; and Lord Wargrave, who was devoted to poetry though he was shrewd enough never to write any, talked by turns of the beauty of Countess Shimna with her singular family likeness to Lady Thyrza O'Keefe; of various moonlit scenes — of Venice, of Constantinople, and the Alhambra, with which, he hinted, he had tender associations of his own; and of various distinguished ladies who, being dead, could never contradict him, and whose acquaintance with himself had caused much romantic disaster, though whether to them or to him he left chivalrously undetermined.

"If I were your age," he said, "I should, instead of being here, be in a boat in Lyncombe harbour watching the lights of the Moshiska. If you want to keep young," he continued, thinking of his own career, and diverging from particular reflections to general, "you should never attempt to marry before you're forty. You should be humbly content till then with women who are married already. You won't," he said, having debated for a moment whether he should give his wisdom a cynical turn or a sentimental— "you won't be disappointed then by expecting too much of marriage. But look. Your butler is at the window. Is he looking for us for family prayers? You have them, I know, on Sundays. On such occasions I never miss being present. I prayed with Brigham Young every night I was in Salt Lake City."

Pole replied that prayers would not be for another hour, and Lord Wargrave found there was time to relapse into sentiment and philosophy. Pole, however, was not responsive; and the very thought of Countess Shimna, for some reason, appeared to have grown wearisome to him.

"You don't," grunted Lord Wargrave, having congratulated him on possessing so fascinating a neighbour, "seem aware of your *bonne fortune.* Young men of the present day have no love, and no religion. They marry at twenty-five, and cease to say prayers at twenty."

"I," said Pole, with a laugh, "at all events, am not married. And as for praying, we shall all of us pray again when a Royal Commission reports upon what to pray to."

"A night like this," said Lord Wargrave, "is a creed and a religion in itself. What makes religion is feeling."

"Yes," replied Pole, "and it lasts while the feeling lasts. Religious belief in these days is a Penelope's web, which is woven by the soul in emotion, and which the mind unweaves in meditation."

"And in spite of the mind," said Lord Wargrave, "the soul weaves it again."

"Is Saul among the prophets?" murmured Pole; and moving away from his companion for a step or two, he looked out over the sea. " And I, too," he said to himself, " have still a religion left me. It is buried, but buried in my heart; and for me it will still live, till memory no longer sits by the holy sepulchre."

CHAPTER X.

TWENTY-FOUR hours later Mrs. Pole's guests had departed, and a new chapter of life was opened at Glenlynn, after the final closing of one which had lasted for sixty years. But, so far as externals went, the immediate future promised to be merely an unbroken prolongation of the past. The sole innovation was that Miss Drake, who was to remain on, had, after much pressing, consented to dine downstairs.

Pole, who for many months had been engaged on the preparation of a Blue-book, in which the results of his long labours were to be summarized, resolved to take every advantage of a seclusion so favourable to work, and finish the volume, by dint of determined application, before the House reassembled for an imminent autumn session. He had already been corresponding about it with his excellent official chief—a retired

manufacturer of stockings, whom the wisdom
of the Tory party had converted into a peer,
under the homely title of Lord Henderson ;
and Lord Henderson, a man of extreme
practical shrewdness, had exhibited an interest in the task, and a keen sense of its
importance, which inspired Pole's resolution
with new vigour and spirit.   There was,
indeed, at present nothing to distract him
from it.   Countess O'Keefe had written to
Mrs. Pole to postpone Countess Shimna's
promised visit for a week, as they were
going with Prince Bobrovski for a cruise
down the coast of Cornwall ; and Pole had
received the news without visible disappoint-
ment. If useful and congenial work, prepared under agreeable circumstances, really
contains, as it is said, the secret of human
happiness, he had apparently every opportunity of working out his own salvation.
His advantages were not merely those of
common quiet and comfort ; they comprised
almost everything calculated to nerve and
gratify the ambition and the faculties of an
energetic man, and caress the feelings of a
sensitive one. Well connected, and bearing
an ancient name, already possessed of a
reputation, intellectual as well as social, and

engaged in an absorbing occupation, which might lead him to a brilliant future, he had not only just succeeded, in the vigorous spring of life, to a beautiful home, which, being his mother's, was his own, but he had also found himself possessed of a private income, so infinitely exceeding his expectations as to seem like a magician's gift. And this new life, despite the suddenness of its advent, joined itself to the old, not with any crude abruptness, but with a noiseless and gentle coalescence, reaching his earliest years with a thousand uniting fibres. Indeed, the rooms and passages, musky with ghosts of departed scents, the old books and the wall-papers, the silver and the flowered china, and the mysterious cupboards into which he had once peeped fearfully, not only brought him back again to his own boyhood, but seemed to exhale upon his spirit the calm of an earlier generation.

It was a calm, too, that was alive with freshness. He would wander out into the early hours before breakfast, when the air was quick with smells of shaven grass; when the scythes swished through the dew on undulating, green declivities; when the flower-

beds were censers, with the soul of the
earth rising from them, and the silver gravel
on the walks rustled beneath his footprints.
He would watch the gardeners, bent by one
lifelong service; their moorland lads beginning the same career, and one or two
wrinkled old women in sun-bonnets, kneeling to grub up weeds. Their very rakes,
and spuds, and wheelbarrows—he had
known them all since childhood. They were
all like objects in prints of a hundred years
ago; and he felt, as he walked alone among
these surroundings, that an unlooked-for
peace was for a time enfolding him in its
wings. This peace even came to possess,
or to simulate, a spiritual character. Dr.
Clitheroe, whose work in that district
was not yet finished, had taken on his
room at the farm for some weeks longer;
whenever he was not absent on business
he had his meals at Glenlynn; and each
morning and evening the gentle inflection
of his voice now filled the dining-room
with the murmur of household prayer. As
Pole knelt and listened to the well-worn
phrases of faith, the heaven, which had
long grown visionary, again appeared above
him, and sheltered him, like a kindly

roof-tree, from the horror of the inhuman Infinite.

But this was not all. Before many days were over, new ideas, new schemes of activity, began to develop themselves in his mind, and revealed sources of happiness to him deeper, in some respects, than any he had known hitherto. Familiar though he had been, and also profoundly interested, in all contemporary problems affecting the prosperity of the masses, and frequent as had been the cases in which, prompted by his kindness, he had given assistance to individual sufferers, his view of the helpless and the suffering had been that of the scientific inquirer, whose business is to supply knowledge to others, rather than set an example by applying it practically himself. Indeed, his position, and the very nature of the duties he had undertaken, had prevented his feeling the existence of any personal relationship between him and the groups of men—themselves so widely separated— whose conditions he studied, and whose evidence he so often took. But now, for the first time in his life, he was no longer a wanderer; and he found himself, in addition to being possessed of a home,

surrounded by human beings, who, instead
of being specimens and examples, had with
that home and himself a vital and a personal
connection.   Intellectually all this was, of
course, a truism to him, of which from the
very first he had been aware; but it was
some days before accident revealed it to him
as a moral truth, and he hardly knew its face
when he looked at it thus transfigured.

He was an active man, accustomed to long
walks; and often, to refresh himself after
work, he would ramble for many miles, re-
newing his boyish acquaintance with the
beautiful country round him.   He thus passed
through several of the moorland villages,
contrasting them with the villages whose
condition he had studied in other countries.
Here the farmers, as he knew, lived in the
patriarchal way, which is, in the West of
England, not even yet extinct.   They worked
with their labourers, and ate often at the
same table with them; and the aspect of
the cottages, and of the simple people themselves, filled him with the feeling that round
the tranquillity of his own home was a zone
of social tranquillity equally undisturbed and
deep.   At first, in fact, they affected his mind
no further than by supplying it with this

sense of passive and almost indolent satisfaction : and he had looked on these scenes
as a pensive observer only, being taken by
the villagers for a tourist who had lost his
way.

But one day when he was struggling to
open an unhinged gate, a woman came out
from a cottage, and civilly offered him her
help. He thanked her with equal friendli-
ness, and was intending to pass on, when he
noticed that on her doorstep a diminutive
child was standing. It was a boy about
three years old, clean and pretty in spite of
its poor clothes. Pole asked the woman if
it was hers. With a smile she answered,
"Yes;" and he, going up to it, patted it
gently on the cheek, and began to talk to it
in very creditable infant English. It looked
up at him as if it had found a friend, and
presently enlivened its half-articulate syllables with that most delightful and mysterious sound—a little child's laughter. Pole
had never, to his own knowledge, possessed
that most valuable gift of conversing easily
with persons out of his own rank of life,
unless there happened to be some definite
reason for doing so ; but now sitting
down on a bench and taking the boy on

his knee, he began to talk to the mother about it, and presently to question her about herself.

At last she said, "You're so good, sir, to my little boy, it may be, perhaps, you've a little boy of your own."

Pole's face saddened. "I am not married," he answered.

"It's not often, sir," said the woman, "that a stranger comes our way. You'll be staying somewhere in these parts, I suppose." He told her who he was. "Indeed, sir!" she exclaimed with a curtsy. "I'm sure I beg your pardon, in case I have been too free."

"I have spent," said Pole, rising, "a very pleasant half-hour with you. I hope I shall see you often. Come, little boy, good-bye. One of these days I shall bring you a pretty top."

He felt as he walked home that suddenly, and without any effort, his knowledge of things had been enlarged by this chance interview; and those roots of life, the simplest human sympathies, were revealed to him pushing their fibres through the whole human soil, and binding together all classes, however otherwise divided.

It so happened that, in an equally accidental way, the same grave fact was forced on him again next morning; only now it was under a different aspect. Close to the home-farm there lived a labourer's family, which was well enough known at Glenlynn as improvident, and always poor. Pole had himself known many of its members, in his childhood; and they and their helpless ways had, during Miss Pole's lifetime, excited disapproving amusement, far more than compassion. Dr. Clitheroe, when he appeared at breakfast, brought news that the father was dying, "And I fear," he said, "that the wife and children will be in a very sad plight."

"The Western's," said Mrs. Pole, with a sigh, "have been a trouble ever since I can remember. The more Miss Pole did for them, the less they did for themselves."

"Well," said Pole, as he sipped his coffee indolently, "I suppose we must sin against our principles and help them once again."

He had taken up one of his letters and was amusing himself by looking at the post-marks, when the Doctor observed casually:

"I was told that they really have nothing to eat at all, and that the children are at the door crying. I have promised to give them a little help myself."

"And has no one," exclaimed Pole, "given them even a crust already? Mother, what can I take? Give me some bread and milk—meat, butter, anything. I will go with it myself this moment."

He rang the bell; the required orders were given; and half an hour later he found himself in the cottage kitchen, dispensing his provisions to the children and the mother also; the hunger of the father having just been appeased for ever. Hitherto he had been conscious of that shrinking from the sight of pain which often makes sensitive men more selfish in action than the callous; and he had even now experienced a momentary nausea on first coming face to face with the slatternliness of the misery he was relieving. But the pleasure of giving relief made him forget all else. The cheeks of the children, squalid with dirt and sores, became delightful to him as he offered each mouth its portion; and the youngest little creature he fed with his own hands, watching the smiles sprout on its lips like mushrooms.

He promised to see what could be done further; and the widow's face was a blessing, which went with him when he turned away.

This incident started him on a career of new activity. The sentimental aspect of the scene he had just witnessed soon passed from his mind; but it left behind it a suddenly awakened sense that some of the very evils whose nature he had been so long studying, were here at his very doors, calling on his experience for a cure; and a resolution leapt to life in him, that he would apply practically to these, the remedies which his observation had shown him to be most successful elsewhere.

He explained his ideas to his mother, who was shrewd enough to see their value, and who promised him her help and sanction in any schemes that might be advisable. He sent for the bailiff, and consulted him as to the best means of ascertaining the exact condition of the poor in the surrounding villages; and with a view to obtaining not only information but counsel, he begged his mother to invite Mr. Godolphin to dinner—him and his wife, and all her array of ribands.

The invitation was sent. Mr. and Mrs. Godolphin came. The dinner was at half-past six, this early hour having been chosen in order that afterwards they might enjoy the evening out-of-doors; and for the same reason, all were in morning dress — Mrs. Godolphin being, for her part, a perfect Golconda of jet beads. After dinner Pole in the twilight garden drew Mr. Godolphin away with him, and began to unfold his plans, which comprised an orphanage, with an industrial school attached, and perhaps a lodging for widows; and explained how such modest institutions had been tried with success in Belgium. He then asked Mr. Godolphin for advice and help, deferring to his practical wisdom, and superior local knowledge.

Mr. Godolphin was not only touched by this appeal, he was flattered by it. But his vanity was of that rare and delightful kind which stimulates its possessor's best qualities only; and he listened with the keenest attention to Pole's plans and prospects, criticizing them at the same time with great practical shrewdness. At last he stopped short in his walk, put his hand upon Pole's shoulder, and looked at him with generous eyes. " I

am thankful," he said, "to see that your
aunt's spirit lives in you." He paused, and
then with a tremor in his voice, continued:
"Canon Bulman was telling me that you
had become a free-thinker. I confess I am
not quite able to tell what that word means.
The more freely I think myself, the more
firmly do I believe in Christ. And, Reginald
—may I call you that? for I knew you when
you were quite a lad — I spoke just now
of your good aunt's spirit living in you. I
ought to have said that what lives in you is
the spirit of Christ; and I will not forbid
you, if in doctrine you should not exactly
follow me."

In width of knowledge, and in intellectual
power generally, Pole was, beyond compari-
son, superior to Mr. Godolphin; but what
most helps and encourages even the greatest
of practical thinkers, what braces the sinews
of their will, and makes its strength a reality
instead of a wasted possibility, is the support
and appreciation of ordinary simple men;
and Pole experienced the reality of this great
truth now. Mr. Godolphin, moreover, possessed, in addition to his simplicity, a
temperament which, in some ways, was as
active as Pole's own. Many men who like

him had spent most of their lives in the
care of the poor, and who had done so, as
no doubt *he* had, with a special, even if
humble, complacency, might have felt some
jealous distrust of a young layman like
Pole, who was thus presuming to intrude
into their own department, and whose
ideas, whatever their value, were an implied
criticism of theirs. But to such feelings as
these, Mr. Godolphin was a total stranger.
Much that Pole said to him was to him
certainly new ; but he welcomed its novelty
as a help, not an insult to himself. In
especial he welcomed Pole's practical suggestion that they should provide themselves
with the large-scale ordnance-maps of the
neighbourhood—maps which showed clearly
each individual cottage, and compile, with
this to guide them, a list as complete
as possible, of the families inhabiting each,
with their wages and condition generally.

Intercourse between Glenlynn and Mr.
Godolphin's vicarage was of daily occur-
rence whilst these preliminaries were being
settled ; and formed for Pole the pleasantest
element in his life. He did not, however,
allow his official work to suffer ; and he

found time also, with the aid of a Lyncombe architect, to make some rough plans
for his proposed simple buildings. His
mother, though hitherto all her ideas of
charity had been nearly as old-fashioned as
those of Miss Pole herself, welcomed his
projects with a sympathy not unlike Mr.
Godolphin's; and meanwhile, in private, he
had resolved on setting aside for these
philanthropic purposes, and for another, more
secret, but equally unselfish, most of that ad-
ditional income which had so unexpectedly
come to him. In this way he was carrying
into action the kind of resolve which his
mind, at Miss Pole's funeral, had laid as an
offering before he knew not what Power;
and the charm of his home, and the interest
of his official work, were supplemented and
increased by a contentment whose source
was deeper.

But in spite of all this, a certain portion
of his being was tenanted by a distress or
melancholy, which work, ambition, the
approval of conscience, and the mere pleasure
of living, might often reduce to silence,
but could not dislodge. To have detected
this fact would have required a far acuter
observer than any of those persons by

whom he now happened to be surrounded, and most of its signs, indeed, were beyond the observation of anybody. But any one who could have watched him in the solitude of his own bedroom, or followed him on the lonely rambles which he every day took, would have seen reason to be convinced that all the liberal sunshine which the outward and inward world had combined to pour on him was constantly made cold and grey by some cloud of anxiety or of sorrow.

Like many men suffering in the same way, he would frequently, when alone, talk aloud to himself in broken sentences. Several times, in the morning, when his letters had been brought to him in bed, he exclaimed, as he looked them over, " Nothing—not a single line!" and this would be succeeded sometimes by some ejaculations such as these—"I have given all I have, and I get not even a word;" "I did not think it was in human nature to be so cruel;" or again, "I feel myself cut off from everything that is best in life, as if I had been a murderer." There was, moreover, a certain path clambering along the heathery cliff-side, to which each day he would betake himself; and, seating himself on a lonely rock, he would look out over the sea, on which now and again some white wave would flower, and which whispered far below, with its foam, upon curves of shingle. From here, high on the horizon the form of a coast was visible, where Wales opened to the Atlantic a succession of visionary forelands; and the eyes of the lonely watcher would fix themselves from time to time on their distant and elusive shadows, which were hardly distinguishable from clouds. Here, too, he would not unfrequently talk to himself, in phrases which were similar to those just mentioned, and which any one who overheard them could not have failed to attribute either to unhappiness of the deepest kind, or else to the most ridiculous affectation of it. That it was not affectation, however, would have been proved sufficiently by the fact that the moment he was in the presence of others, his demeanour entirely altered, and he assumed the appearance of equable, and often of buoyant spirits. His aspect, indeed, would brighten occasionally even when he was alone, as though the natural hunger for happiness, inherent in a sensitive and vigorous nature, would insist on satisfying itself, despite all opposition from the mind; and he would view the scenes around him with the pleasure which is characteristic of a poet, and which is heightened, rather than disturbed, by a melancholy which has lost its sting.

Cloudless intervals like these were the result and the reward usually of some exceptionally hard, or exceptionally successful work, whether this were connected with his Blue-book or his philanthropic projects; and after ten days or so of life under his present circumstances, there came to him a morning of work that was exceptional in both ways. A letter from his chief, Lord Henderson, was brought to him, when he was still in bed, begging him to send, by return of post, if possible, certain comparative tables with regard to artisans' house-rent in Paris, Berlin, and other continental towns. As the first post left at one, and it was desirable to catch this, he ordered his breakfast to be brought him in his own room, and working there without intermission, just finished his task in time. This close application happened to be all the easier to him because a succession of light showers deprived him of any temptation to go out. But when he was placing the document in its envelope, he saw that the sky was clearing, and he rose, rejoicing in the prospect of a half-hour's stroll before luncheon.

He was, however, a little surprised when Miss Drake, whom he encountered in the hall, congratulated him on this change in the weather, with what seemed a disproportionate emphasis; and it also occurred to him, when he came to think it over, that her face was starched into an expression of unusual preciseness, and that the body of her black dress was unusually rich in crape. But these reflections quickly passed away from him as he went into the open air and smelt the soil of the garden in it, and saw about him the soft silvery mist assuming the dazzling whiteness that breaks into blue and gold. He forgot his statistics; he forgot all definite sorrow; and his mind for the moment became a garden of hopes and feelings, vague and delightful as the scenes of the garden round him. All those feelings which the beauty of Nature, as distinct from her grandeur, touches in us, are connected directly or indirectly with religion, or else with love; and to Pole, who had known romance, it seemed that the flower-scented

air around him held vague, diaphanous
memories, without passion or regret in them,
of women who had charmed him, and of the
scenes that had been impregnated with
their presence. His mind thus pleasurably
agitated, he was strolling, almost heedless
of where he went, down one of the little
walks that descended tortuously to the shore,
when the bough of a rose-tree, bent with its
weight of moisture, arrested his course,
stretching across his pathway like a bar. It
was bright with blossoms, and he stood still
to look at them. His gaze lost itself in the
depth of the crumpled shadows, where far
down were flickerings as of diamonds in
crimson caves; and in every drop that was
globed on the upper petals, he detected a
miniature universe of colour and leaf and
sky. From this state of contemplation a
sound of footsteps roused him. They seemed
to be near at hand, but he could not distinguish where. He hastily raised the
branch and proceeded as the path led him,
hoping to avoid a meeting with anybody—
even with his mother. A yard or two lower
down the path took a sharp bend, and brought
him to a view of the sea, framed in an arch
of trellis-work. The waves shone in streaks

of purple and of green turquoise; high in the
air the arch was a curve of passion flowers,
and beyond were rocks and myrtle, and the
spikes of one large grey aloe. It was a view
for which he entertained a special affection,
seeming to unite, as it did, the beauties both
of Italy and of England. But, in addition to
these, it revealed to him another beauty now,
which brought him to a surprised stand-
still. This was nothing else than Countess
Shimna O'Keefe, with a figure daintier than
any that Watteau dreamed of, and a dress
redolent of the sea, as the sea is understood
at Deauville. During the whole morning
the thought of her had not so much as
crossed his mind; but, on seeing her, he
remembered that she was expected to-day
for luncheon, and he realized all at once,
with a certain sensation of amusement, the
true explanation of Miss Drake's aspect and
demeanour. He was sure that she had been
alarmed by the Canon's description of the
stranger, and he augured that the reality
would alarm her even more.

But this faint sensation of amusement was
not his sole experience. For a moment his
face grew grave, as he thought of how he
had met this stranger last, and how her hand

had lingered in his on the landing-steps of the Lyncombe pier : and shame at the interest she had excited in him passed through him like a shuddering spirit, whose place was again taken by the very interest which its passage had reproved.

CHAPTER XI

COUNTESS SHIMNA at first was not aware of his presence. With an absorbed attention she was looking at the scene before her, and the simplicity of her attitude and expression was rendered doubly striking by contrast with her toilette, which, though in its own way equally simple, betrayed in every detail the subtleties of Parisian art. For a few seconds Pole had time to watch her. Then she started and saw him, and he came forward to meet her. Their greeting, so far as words went, consisted of inevitable commonplaces. He hoped she had not been rained upon, during her miniature voyage from Lyncombe, and they congratulated each other on the fact that the weather had so completely cleared. But meanwhile he was receiving impressions of her which had little to do with what she uttered. Her skin and complexion, free from the least

trace of cosmetics, had yet the unnatural
daintiness of a face on an old French fan;
and her English, though perfect, had yet the
faintest of foreign accents, which made it
like Sèvres china, as contrasted with common
ware. Her touch, too, once more thrilled him
with its almost unconscious lingering, and
her dress, as he looked more closely at it,
roused a new train of associations in him.
Various points in it, for which, man-like, he
had no name, ambushed coquetries of colour
and fit and fold, filled him with thoughts of
far-off continental dissipation, of the glitter
of casinos, and of whisperings under lamp-lit
foliage. But thoughts and impressions like
these were at once chastened and intensified
by others of a different order. If much in
her air and aspect suggested an artificial
world, in her face, as she looked at him, was
an almost tragic sincerity. Her upper lip
had a certain lift in its curve, as if she were
ready to gasp with acute feeling; and the
look of her eyes was that of a heart's-ease
wet with morning.

"I am glad I met you," she said, when the
first civilities were over. "I should have
been shy of making my way to a strange
house all alone."

Any man who has been accustomed to deal with women, and has shared with them the beginnings and endings of a certain class of experiences, may have divided himself, as far as possible, from his past by change of ideas and conduct; but whenever he meets a woman whose history has been similar to his own, the past of each has the inevitable and unsought effect of producing between the two an unrecognized, and even unconscious, freemasonry. The man's knowledge of other women becomes knowledge of this one, and the woman is endowed similarly with an instinctive knowledge of the man. Pole, though he was no more aware of the fact than of the tone of his own voice, was himself an example of this truth now. He looked at Countess Shimna without a trace of freedom or familiarity, and yet he spoke to her as most men would not have spoken to such a stranger.

"I confess," he said, "I should never have thought you shy. You seem to me like a most perfect woman of the world."

She returned his look with a sparkle of quiet comprehension between her eyelashes.

"Of one world, yes," she said; "but not of a world like this. You may not know it,

Mr. Pole, but to-day is a great day for me.
For the first time in my life I shall be entering an English home. I am half English
myself. English governesses have educated
me. I have read English books — poetry,
philosophy, novels — all of it ; and I know, or
think I know, what an English home must
be. That is what makes me shy. Or suppose that I tell you plainly — I feel shy of
your mother."

"Why?" asked Pole, watching her as she
dropped her eyes and played with a sleeve-
link formed out of two black pearls.

"There are many reasons," she answered,
as if she were addressing the gravel —
"reasons I can't explain. But here is one,
and that one is quite simple. She represents
a life in which I have no part."

"You have met me only twice," said Pole,
"and you are not shy of *me*."

"No," she said; "but you are different.
Would you like me," she continued, laughing, "to tell you what I mean by that? I
have, as you say, met you only twice. How
do I know you are different? How do I
know what you are? I can tell you in an
original way. In a Warsaw newspaper,
which we got yesterday morning — you know

the stupid things that are always coming in
newspapers — was a letter stating that the
eye retains, after death, the picture of whatever object it looked at last when living.
That, of course, is nonsense; but there is
something like it which is true. Eyes which
have been familiar with certain sides of
life, retain an expression produced by what
they have seen; and other eyes, which
have seen the same things, recognize it.
I recognize something like this in you—in
your whole expression — no matter what
you look at, whether at a funeral service, or at this garden, or—you must not
think me a coquette because I say this—or
at myself."

"I am glad," said Pole, "that you feel me
to have something in common with you;
but I should like to think that the feeling
rested on anything rather than the fact that
your past had been like mine."

"My present is like yours, at any rate,"
she replied, looking slowly round her. "We
are both of us seeing the same side of life
now. Is your home as beautiful as your
garden?"

"Come," he said—"come and see. I am
glad, at any rate, that you like my favourite

view.   Look at those colours that float upon our western sea."

"Ah!" she answered, sighing, as if entering into his mood instantly; "that *nuance* of blue, far out!   I have been looking at it all the way from Lyncombe."

They now moved away, and she followed him up one of the climbing paths, he apologizing for its unsociable narrowness and its difficulty.

"Ah," she exclaimed, as if nothing but trifles had passed between them, "here is your house!   I can see the roofs and chimneys."

At this moment the sound of his own name reached Pole through one of the laurel hedges, and presently, at the end of the path, he caught sight of his mother, who called to him a little out of breath—

"Reginald, I've been looking for you everywhere.   I wanted to ask you to meet Countess Shimna at the landing-place."

"Mother," he said, "she is here."

With a slight gesture of surprise Mrs. Pole looked beyond him, and scanned for an instant the delicate figure facing her.

"My dear," she exclaimed, "I've been wishing so much to see you."

"And I, too," said Countess Shimna, "have been wishing so much to come."

Pole watched her curiously. He saw how she had advanced with a kind of calm timidity, far more finished in its *aplomb* than any possible boldness, and he said to himself, "If this is shyness, it is shyness become a fine art." But then, on his mother's speaking to her, he saw all her expression change, and its dainty conventionality became transfigured into childlike gratitude. He saw the change go home to his mother's heart. He saw the gentle curve of the girl's lips appeal to her, and, bending with a maternal welcome, the elder woman kissed the younger.

"My dear," said Mrs. Pole, "you look like a living flower. With you on its walks, our garden will hardly know itself. Hark! that bell means luncheon—what you, I suppose, call *déjeuner*. Come and see how your English relations live."

Pole followed them, delighted at the success of the meeting, and very soon he saw, under his mother's influence, an entirely new side of Countess Shimna's nature show itself.

"You will find," Mrs. Pole said to her as

they drew near the front door, "me and my son alone, except for one other person, a strange old *dame de campagnie;*" and she then proceeded to give a description of Miss Drake. "I've no doubt," she continued, "you've seen a great many things and people, but I am sure you have never seen anything in the least like her."

Countess Shimna stood still and broke into a ripple of laughter, which showed her hearers that, whatever she had seen or not seen, she grasped the idea of Miss Drake, and saw her with her mind's eye now. Her appreciation was so unexpected, and the effect of her mirth was so contagious, that her laughter was joined in directly by the two others, until Mrs. Pole said, "Hush! It would never do if she were to hear us." And they passed indoors into the hall.

"Ah," said Countess Shimna softly, as at Mrs. Pole's suggestion she laid down her sunshade, with a parrot's head for a handle, on the cool surface of an old marble table, and glanced at the busts, at the glimmering china bowls, and the carpet mellowed with its hundred years of wear, "this is what I knew a home would be."

"Look," whispered Pole. "There Miss Drake is."

And there, sure enough, in an inner hall she was, illuminated by the staircase window and standing at an open door, as if waiting for the others to pass into the drawing-room before her. As they did so, Mrs. Pole introduced the Countess, and Miss Drake dropped a short curtsy, which resembled the collapse of a concertina. Limited as the social powers of this estimable lady were, she contributed more than any one to make luncheon pass off easily. One of her earliest emotions had been horror of the first Napoleon, and she still clung to the idea that everybody not English was French. Countess Shimna had read of people like this in books ; and nothing could exceed her delight at coming across a living specimen. She divined at once that in Miss Drake's eyes she was a Frenchwoman ; and drawing her out in the prettiest way imaginable, had at last the satisfaction of hearing herself asked if frogs were not, when one ate them, exactly like skinny chicken. Miss Drake, in fact, promoted conversation much in the same way that a cat, a dog, or a child does, to whom everybody conspires to talk. She had never been the recipient of so much attention before, and indeed of the pleasure she caused she was herself perhaps the chief participator. Unwonted smiles made novel wrinkles along her cheeks. Her curls, which were so prim this morning, now frisked with satisfaction; and the outlandish young lady, who she fancied would smell of brimstone, seemed to her by the end of luncheon little less than an angel. But opinions suddenly changed are proverbially unstable. As the party were on the point of rising, out of the corners of her provincial eyes Miss Drake saw Countess Shimna take her gloves from her lap—long, delicate gloves, with hands that were yet more delicate; and she felt a sudden shock at the girl's physical beauty. It seemed wicked to her, like some strange form of luxury. Then in an instant came another shock worse than this one. She recollected that this alien must be a Roman Catholic, and a worshipper of saints and idols. Her mouth grew rigid with religious and moral Protestantism; and as soon as they left the dining-room she fled to her own chamber.

"My dear," said Mrs. Pole, as she took her guest into the library, "I have a few letters to write, which I could not finish this morning. I will get them off my hands now, and return to you with a clear conscience. Meanwhile I will leave you to the care of Reginald."

She went, closing the door. Pole and Countess Shimna were alone.

"Well," he said to her, with a look full of the questions that grow only from the soil of a mutual understanding. To his considerable astonishment he saw gathering in her eyes, not actual tears, but the dimness that comes before them.

"I should," she said, "love your mother, if only I knew her better."

"I know her," said Pole; "and she is devoted to you already." His manner was different from what it had been in the morning. There was for the moment nothing in it but simple responsive friendship. "Tell me," he went on, "do you like our home also?"

She began to look slowly round her, taking in every object, like a person who is half stifled, inhaling a draught of air. "Being here," she said, "is like being in church. Your house surrounds me, as a church does, with a life unlike my own, and there is some quiet of old times floating in the air like incense. You won't know what I mean when I say that. You will laugh at me; but I am made up of nerves and senses; and with me one sense is always speaking for another. Do you understand that? One of my governesses used to tell me I mixed my metaphors. For me, scents speak, colours sound, and sounds flash like colour."

"Well," replied Pole, "come and see how the colours are sounding out-of-doors." And a moment or two later they went out together into the summer. The golden air was fresh with a wayward breeze, that came in sighing puffs from every quarter indifferently, and seemed to be laden with the spirit of moorland honey. "This," said the girl, "is all a new life to me. I have felt nothing exactly like it before—so lonely, so civilized, and yet so free." She seemed to Pole to understand the place as he did. He watched her with a curious interest, delighted to see her happy.

As they went they began talking of various matters. She mentioned that she had noticed in the library the works of some of her favourite writers — of Byron and Shelley amongst the number, and of one or two men of science—these last being volumes which

Pole had himself brought down. "I saw
'*Werther*,' too," she said; "but that is silly
and morbid — and Wordsworth. My first
governess used to make me learn his verses."

The extent of her reading surprised him;
and still more than her reading, the way in
which she had made her own the intellectual
meanings of most of it, so that they mixed
themselves with her lightest thoughts, and
moved familiarly with them. He hardly
made an allusion to which she did not
respond. She caught what he said as if it
had been a ball tossed to her; and sometimes her mind, as through it his thoughts,
came back to him, seemed like a prism
which had dyed them with deeper colours.

"See," she exclaimed, as a turn in one of
the walks gave her a new view of the singular
and precipitous garden, "there is the wild
heather shining above the lawns and
laurels!"

"I will take you to it," he answered; "you
shall lie on it. But you must not mind a
climb."

He led her up walks that mounted through
sloping thickets of laurustinus. They left
the garden; they passed through a wood of
larches, and presently found themselves on

the slanting wilderness of the cliffs. From
the heights of the rocks above them down
to the waves below, was heather, stretching
before them in miles of headlong purple.
Here and there on a crag some mountaineer-
ing sheep glittered; and above them a sea-
gull passed, like the drifting petals of a
magnolia. "The heather is dry," said Pole.
"Try it: it is a bed of velvet."

She sank down amongst the tufts, with the
supple gracefulness of a fawn; only as she
did so, from her dress came a breath of
perfume, which again in Pole's mind connected her with a far-off artificial civilization.
He sat himself on a stone close by. The
heather had half hidden her.

"From where you are," he said, "you can
see nothing."

"On the contrary," she answered, laughing,
"I can see an entire world. I can see—shall
I tell you what? I can see little flowers—a
nation of them—yellow, and white, and blue,
showing me their faces through the grass.
On each side of me is the heather like great
hills. I can count the lights and shadows
streaking the highest bells; and beyond these
is the sky. And now I am looking in front of
me. There my heather hills dip into an

inverted triangle; and this is filled up by a lilac wall of sea. And I smell the earth. Ah!" she exclaimed, raising herself, "why should we consider it a reproach to be called of the earth, earthy? Why should we be ashamed of a parent through whom the violets are our sisters?"

When they re-entered the house, Mrs. Pole was still upstairs. They went into the silent library, where the blinds, which were now drawn down, filled the room with a cool luminous dimness. Her face and eyes, seen in this different light, startled Pole by their expression of meditative melancholy. He went up close to her, where she stood in an undecided attitude, and said, "Will you do me a favour? Will you turn round to the light? Thank you. Forgive me for staring at you. Come with me, and I will now show you the reason."

Not unnaturally puzzled, she followed him into the room adjoining. There he surprised her further. He seized her arm abruptly, and led her to the pastel portrait. "Look at that," he said. "Perhaps you will understand now."

For some moments she stared at the picture silently; then, hastily turning to him,

"Do you mean," she exclaimed, "that is like me?" He took from a table a little ivory looking-glass and put it into her hand for answer. She looked alternately at the picture and her own reflection, and at last said, "Who is she?"

"She is," replied Pole, "some distant relation of both of us. But the thing so like yourself in her is the whole air and the expression."

"It is strange," she said, looking at the picture, and evidently not displeased at the thought of its being associated with herself— "it is strange how likenesses are handed down in families: and I suppose our characters, our feelings, even our little half-thought thoughts, have their family likenesses in just the same way—only likenesses to counterparts which nobody ever knew or painted. I often wonder which of my thoughts are my own, and which are echoes from my ancestors. Do you know these verses? I think you must. They express what I feel, in this way, with regard to my own nature sometimes.

'"Will no man tell me what she sings?
    Perhaps the numbers flow,
  From old unhappy far-off things,
    And battles long ago.'"

My governess I told you of, made me learn
that.   But the portrait—— You didn't tell
me what the name of the lady was."

"The lady," said Pole, "was the celebrated Lady Thyrza Brancepeth. She ran
away with the man who built this house
—my great-uncle. She died only a year
afterwards. She is mentioned in Byron's
Letters."

Countess Shimna sank into a chair, with
her eyes still fixed upon the picture. "Yes,"
she said presently, "she died in Italy. And
so that was your great-uncle!" For a
few moments she was silent. Then she
spoke again. "I am amused," she said,
at your asking me if I ever heard the story.
Some day I can show you a picture which
has a story also. I can show you a miniature of lady Thyrza Brancepeth's daughter.
You will not wonder then why I should be
like that picture. If you care for science,
you ought to be pleased to see me. Judging
from that picture, I am a good instance
of atavism. See," she said, interrupting
herself with a laugh, "I have dropped
my pocket-handkerchief." He picked it up
for her. A curve of her lips thanked him.
"Consider," she said, smiling, as if to escape

from seriousness, whilst her gloved fingers
played with the film which she called
her handkerchief, " consider the things of
which I am the child, or rather the great-
grandchild—of elopement, and of sorrow, and
of passion, and of early death. My shield
has all those *quartiers* to make up for the
one that is wanting."

Pole looked at her, puzzled and fascinated.
He could not tell what to make of her.
How, he asked himself, did she come by
thoughts like these—this flower of an idle
world, who by turns seemed bud and
blossom ; and who sat there brilliant among
the faded colourings of the room, with lips
that were like a kiss, and eyes that were
like an elegy. But the last words were
hardly uttered, when he saw her expression
alter, and the dancing light of childhood
leapt back again into her face. Before he
had himself perceived it, Mrs. Pole had
entered, and coming to Countess Shimna,
laid a gentle hand upon her shoulder. " You
are not tired?" she said. "Ah, here comes
Martin with the tea. But now tell me this.
Your mother, of course, will allow you to
stay to dinner? The nights are warm, and
the launch will go back on moonlight."

It struck Pole as a strange, incongruous thing to hear their guest questioned about a mother's permission; and yet, when he saw how her face was suffused with childish pleasure, as she told Mrs. Pole that she was perfectly free to stay, she again seemed to him to be a mere child, after all. This impression was presently completed, when the figure of Miss Drake appeared, and grim with shyness, advanced slowly towards the group, moving along the carpet like a clockwork mouse on wheels. Countess Shimna's face lit up again with the light of a half-mischievous amusement; and Miss Drake's lips and cheeks had presently crackled into smiles which showed that this daughter of Heth had made her once more a captive.

After tea, Mrs. Pole proposed to Countess Shimna a drive in a pony carriage up the long approach; "Which will show you," she said, "how we are shut out from the world. The carriage holds only two. Reginald will perhaps ride." It was done as Mrs. Pole suggested. Pole, on an Exmoor pony, for most of the way followed them at a little distance, so as to let his mother and her guest cement their friendship by themselves;

and he listened with puzzled pleasure
to their soft intimate laughter. On their
way back, when they had almost reached
the house, they came upon Dr. Clitheroe,
trudging from his lodgings, washed and
arrayed for dinner, and carrying in his
hand a little paper parcel. "Stop!" cried
Pole, to his mother. "I want to introduce
him to the Countess. Dr. Clitheroe, here is
a lady who has never known an English
clergyman, though she has had the privilege,
I think, of seeing you once in the garden."

"I wish," said the Doctor, as he raised his
dignified hat, "that the Countess saw before
her a worthier member of his profession,
Mrs. Pole," he continued shyly, still glancing at her companion. "I have brought
you a present—one of those little patent
strainers, for fixing to the spout of a teapot,
and catching the leaves."

"How delightful," exclaimed Countess
Shimna, amused by him as she had been
at Miss Drake. "Dr. Clitheroe, how
delightful!"

The Doctor, like Mrs. Pole, was already a
victim to her charm; and at dinner his conversation displayed a demure sparkle, by
which poor Miss Drake was eclipsed, and

which came as a surprise to everybody. Whatever else might be in Countess Shimna's nature, there was one thing in it, at all events, that was completely genuine —the buoyancy of spontaneous girlhood, mischievous without being malicious, caressing even in its audacities, perfectly trained by the world, and yet supremely natural. She forced on Pole the impression of a child adorned with diamonds, which became her and increased her beauty because she was quite unconscious that she was wearing them.

But by-and-by when the time came for her to go, and, when wrapped in a fur-lined cloak that had been sent up to her from the launch, she went out alone with him, and they found themselves in the scented night, his impression of her changed suddenly. She was once again for him a woman, as she had been when he met her in the morning, with whom, in virtue of her past, he was conscious of some undefined intimacy. Her eyes said it, as they looked at him, dim and liquid in the moonlight. Her lips themselves could hardly have been more eloquent, no matter how she had used them: and when they spoke her voice was in harmony with her whole bearing. "You must help me every part of the way," she said; and quietly took his arm.

The effect of this slight action was to fill him with a fantastic jealousy. How had she learned to take a man's arm so easily? What other man—what other men—had taught her? Such was the question he asked himself till the sense of her hand leaning on him, reminded him that he, at all events, possessed this treasure now, and showed him also that his support was not by any means superfluous. The sloping paths and the broken lights and shadows were enough to make his guidance necessary; and until they were close upon the shore he had hardly opened his lips to her, except to say briefly, "You will come to us soon again?" For a second, as he said this, she leaned on his arm more heavily. So at least he thought. If so, it was her only answer. But now when the waves were glimmering within a few yards of them, and they heard the spitting of steam from the launch by the rude landing-place, she paused in her walk, she turned to him, and she took his hand. "Would you like to see me again?" she said. "Perhaps you had better not; but by-and-by, if your mother asks me, I will come. For two strangers, I think, we know each other very well. And now—you must not hold me. Come, help me on board, and make quite sure that you have got rid of me."

She hardly needed his help, she stepped into the boat so lightly. The screw churned the darkness. Water began to gleam between them. She raised her hand, until— so he fancied—it nearly touched her lips; then she waved it in his direction—about this there could be no doubt; and he watched her drifting away from him over the wattled black and silver.

The house, when he returned to it, seemed to be unusually quiet; and himself disinclined to talk, he took up the day's papers, which, until that moment, he had not found time to glance at. His eyes wandered over the columns carelessly, till at last he leaned towards the light, and made the whole sheet rustle, as his attention was quite accidentally caught by the following paragraph.

"Amongst the passengers last Saturday by the 'Umbria' for New York, was Sir Hugh

Price Masters, who succeeded recently to the baronetcy, and to the ownership of St. Owen's Castle, one of the most curious though least visited of the historic mansions of Great Britain. Sir Hugh, who has been long known in sporting circles, and who fractured his thigh last year, when riding Gallipot at Frankfort, is understood to have some big venture afoot in the United States, which, since he is acting in conjunction with Mr. Julius K. Van Skink, we may, though the nature of the project hitherto has been kept dark, conclude to be not unconnected with the noble animal horse."

This elegant piece of literature was enough for Pole that evening. It did for him what could have been done by no other piece of literature in the house. It completely put out of his head the events of the last nine hours: and it certainly was not of Countess Shimna that he was thinking, when he muttered as he went to bed, " And has she gone too! Gone, and without a single word !"

CHAPTER XII.

HE passed a restless night; but towards morning slept so heavily that when his servant brought him his letters, he had some difficulty in rousing himself, or in seeing distinctly what had been put into his hand. At last, however, he perceived on one of the envelopes, an address in untidy, but by no means weak, handwriting. As if something had stung him, he started up in his bed, and staring at the address again, broke the envelope open. The words written were few, being nothing more than these—

"Laburnum Lawn, Windsor.
"My Dear Mr. Pole,
        "I deserve anything you can say of me. I am an abominable correspondent. But lately I could not have written, I have been so busy; though you won't believe me. I had to come to London with my husband,

who has gone back to America; but I
have been so knocked up and ill, with
what I have had to do at the Castle, that
I have come down here for quiet. I shall
stay here for a fortnight, unless I am wanted
at home before. I am in lodgings. If you
should be in London, do run down and see
me, on any day that is convenient to you.
Post is going. No time for more. I am
ever your sincere friend,

" Pansy."

He read this twice, then leapt from his
bed, and his face as he entered the breakfast
parlour, where Dr. Clitheroe was finishing
prayers, had a look of eager pleasure upon
it, that was tempered by vague sadness.
The Doctor, however, was shadowed by no
such cloud. He rose from his knees, and
closed Bishop Bloomfield's manual, which,
with much ingenuity, he had been propping
up against the sugar basin, bright and
twinkling as if he had been getting out of
his bath ; and as soon as he had said " Good
morning," he remarked, with much Christian
briskness, on the manifold charms of the
young lady who had last night been dining
with them. Mrs. Pole, too, seemed to be

in quite as good spirits as the Doctor; and
she, like him, was still full of Countess
Shimna.

"I am so glad to hear," she said, "that
she is going to be left at Lyncombe. I told
her she had better come here; and so she
will for a day or two. But the doctors
advise her that bracing air is what she
wants, and insist on her being established
high up on the cliff."

"By all means," said Pole, with an indifference that surprised his mother. "Let
her come when it best suits her. But till
next Wednesday I myself shall probably be
away. I have just had a letter which will
oblige me to go to London to-morrow."

"Very well, then," said Mrs. Pole; "we
will ask her to come next week. By the
way," she continued, "I have heard from
Ethel De Souza. She and Mrs. Steinberg
have just come back to Thames Wickham.
Perhaps you will go and see them. You will
not find many friends in London."

"Indeed!" exclaimed Pole, with animation.
"Of all women in the world, Mrs. Steinberg
is the kindest, and Miss Ethel De Souza the
most gifted. The one is a genius in friendship; the other a genius in every way. These,

Dr. Clitheroe, are friends whom we first knew in Paris.   Steinberg and De Souza were the great Brazilian bankers.   Miss De Souza is Mrs. Steinberg's niece. She is an orphan, and keeps house with her aunt.   Mrs. Steinberg, mother, has so often asked me to stay with them, that I think I will telegraph to her, and ask her if they can have me now."

A message was despatched accordingly; and in due time came an answer. "To-morrow, by all means; it will be, indeed, a pleasure."

Early next morning he started, and was speeding along the high coach-road, whilst the dews and the gossamers were still glittering on the gorse, and the purple dyes of night were wet on the distant hills.   The sight of a train was strange to him, after the quiet seclusion of Glenlynn; but his thoughts were already travelling faster than steam could carry them.   It seemed to him that the London express, for which he had to wait at a junction, would never come; and he looked down the line impatiently.   At last he saw in the distance a something like a slim black horse-shoe, cut against the sky, with pennon of white fluttering from it—a something that seemed to enlarge, but not to

advance nearer; until, with a sudden sound,
it swelled to a hissing engine; and the train
came sweeping in with its roaring wall of
windows.

His journey, it so happened, was not
without incident. When he reached Reading, at which station he was to change, his
attention was caught by a considerable bustle
on the platform, taking place in front of a
carriage near that he had just left. There
was a group—or a little crowd—of men, well-
dressed in black, clustering eagerly round the
door of a first-class compartment. Some
of them were evidently clergymen; whilst
those, who as evidently were not so, rivalled
their reverend brethren in the edifying gravity
of their demeanour. In another moment
there were bowings and a great shaking
of hands; and over one clerical wide-awake,
whose wearer had the stature of Zaccheus,
Pole perceived the well-known countenance
of Canon Bulman, florid with recognition of
the distinguished welcome he was receiving,
but stamped at the same time with a look
that portended business. As the circle of his
admirers opened to allow of his being conducted out of the station, he happened to
perceive Pole; and quitting his companions,

came up to him. Flushed with the many successes which he had achieved since he left Glenlynn, Canon Bulman was determined to make one effort more at reducing Pole to his former flattering allegiance, or, at all events, to show himself to him in all the pomp of victory.

"My dear boy," he exclaimed, with a geniality almost patronizing, "I'm delighted to see you—quite delighted! Are you stopping in this neighbourhood? If you are, I wish you would come to-night and hear my address on 'Democracy and Personal Purity.'"

Pole explained the reason why this pleasure would be impossible for him.

"Then come," said the Canon, "and lunch with me at my new house to-morrow or the day after. I'm only just out of Windsor, and you can reach me from Thames Wickham easily."

This invitation Pole cordially accepted, promising that that evening he would send the Canon a telegram ; and presently, as he renewed his journey, in spite of other thoughts that had been occupying him, he began to give his mind to the friends whom he was so fast approaching. His early acquaintance with Mrs. Steinberg had been

kept up by him ever since; and her niece for
the last ten years he had known intimately
also. Miss De Souza was indeed a remarkable woman. Born amongst surroundings
the very essence of which was luxury—the
sort of luxury that aims at turning all life
into a bon-bon box tied with ribbons and
lined with quilted satin, and herself by no
means free from a certain sensuous appreciation of it, her existence had yet been that
of a spirit in a world of matter. A singular
quickness of insight, which outran curiosity,
and had very little to do with it, had early
revealed to her, almost against her will, the
realities of human nature; and a gift of
sympathy, equally quick and delicate, had
taken her through the shadows, where others
sinned or suffered, purifying what it touched
of impure, not defiled by it. And yet, little
as her friends suspected it, she had been
herself a victim, not, indeed, to the sins
which she looked on with such cleanly pity,
but to one of those sorrows to which she
seemed to be so superior. Wise for others,
she had at one time been simple for herself;
and her heart, having been left unguarded,
because she had never imagined it to be in
danger, had been yielded up by her almost

without a struggle to the last man in the world
who would have seemed calculated to attract
her. Her own tastes and feelings were to the
highest degree intellectual and sensitive. He
was a soldier and sportsman—a son of the
open air, with little to recommend him to the
eye of ordinary observation, except gallantry
and a semblance of reckless frankness. He
had, however, as events showed, a certain
fastidiousness of taste, with which few of his
friends would have credited him. Captivated
by Miss De Souza, who, besides being wealthy,
well-dressed, and distinguished by much
mundane charm, was also in many ways
beautiful, he had also experienced a genuine
desire for her affection, which appealed to
him as something mysterious and indefinitely
above himself, and which roused him for a
time into a state of stupid adoration. But
no sooner had she, who, if she gave her heart
at all, was a woman to give without reser-
vation or distrust, surrendered to him the
treasure that had lately seemed so inacces-
sible, than he little by little began to dis-
regard and weary of it; and their engagement, which had not been made public, was
barely a month old, before his conduct had
forced on her the invidious responsibility of

dissolving it.   Availing himself of the excuse
thus given him for posing as the aggrieved
party, he engaged himself a month later to
a wealthier woman, whom he married ; and
thus this secret episode in Miss De Souza's
life ended, except for its effects upon herself,
which were not suspected by even her
closest friends, and which she never mentioned to any human being. The sole outward
sign was an increased sympathy for others.

The image of this charming friend was
occupying Pole's mind, and bringing to it a
sense of rest, when the train stopped ; and
he was roused from his reverie by his
servant, who appeared at the carriage door,
and informed him that they had reached
Thames Wickham. A few minutes later, an
open suburban fly, as dirty and as old as any
that had figured at Miss Pole's funeral, was
wheeling out of the dusty road, and convey-
ing him between tall brick gate-posts, into a
space of turf and gravel which was shadowed
by old cedars, and revealed beyond the cedars
the pillars of a large portico. The vehicle drew
up before a flight of wide stone steps ; and
the bell had been hardly rung before double
doors were opened ; and a footman, the
excellence of whose place was visible in his

mien and movements, was vying with Pole's own man in assisting the visitor to descend. Pole glanced about him with the natural curiosity of a new-comer. There slumbered on every object the bloom of a placid opulence. The house was old as suburban villas go, having been built by a Lord Mayor during the reign of George II. But although its exterior, which structurally had been hardly changed, formed still a fine specimen of the stately taste of that period, it was so well coated with paint and shone with such bright plate-glass, that it suggested the last spring-cleaning far more than the last century. A corresponding impression was produced also by the interior. The ceilings, the mahogany doors, and the curving stone staircase, were indeed left much as they had been; but the walls were modern with all the white and gold, that the most florid of contemporary decorators could muster courage to put on them. The old oak floors had been covered with new velvet carpet; and Pole, as he entered the vestibule, saw through two *portières* the fronds of palms distending themselves in the central hall of palms.

A large consequential butler, who was as

well stuffed as a pincushion, and whose
slightest gesture was a compound of a reverence and a benediction, having taken Pole's
hat from him, as an acolyte takes a priest's
vestment, conducted him past the palm trees,
and a retinue of candelabra, into the drawing-room, and left him with the solemn
information that the ladies would be there
presently. Pole, though he had known his
hostesses so well, and for such a long time,
had never till now, visited them in their
present home, which they had indeed acquired only within the last five years. The
general decoration of the house he had taken
in at a glance; and he had recognized with
a smile the profuse spirit of Mrs. Steinberg.
She, as he knew, had been cradled in the
financial world, and her taste, as here exhibited, was an embodied chapter of her
biography. He was aware, however, as he
looked more carefully round him, that other
tastes of a very different order also showed
themselves by abundant signs everywhere.
When his eyes had grown accustomed to
the ormolu clocks and china, and to the
many-coloured satin chairs that were quilted
and stuffed like bon-bon boxes, he realized
that, on every table where china or flowers

left space for them, books and reviews of various kinds were lying; and standing by a piano, at one end of the room, was a harp— that instrument whose shape in itself is music. Moving from table to table, he began glancing at the volumes, all of which evidently lay there for daily use; and these, too, made in his mind an intellectual music of their own. Mrs. Steinberg herself was a woman of talent and cultivation; but the mental musician Pole knew was her niece.

He was absorbed in these impressions when one of the doors was pushed open, and Mrs. Steinberg appeared, shining with smiles and welcome, and cased in black satin, which did justice to her exuberant outlines. She was a woman whom few people had ever looked at without liking. The upper part of her profile suggested that of a parrot, and also a parentage not entirely English; but its keenness was softened by a considerable number of chins, which would constantly send their contours far up into her cheeks; and she looked like what she was—an un-ruined spendthrift in benevolence.

"Ah!" she exclaimed, opening her eyes wide, and prolonging the syllable, till a dozen greetings were comprised in it, "and here you are at last! I have posted back at such a pace—and on foot too—to receive you. I was really so touched by your kindness in thinking of us, and proposing yourself as you did. And how is your sweet mother? and that dear old man, Lord Henderson? I knew him well when he was quite a little humble lad. And I hope you had luncheon in the train, or else you must be completely famished. But tea will come immediately. Hark—I can hear the cups—such a clatter that second footman makes with them."

All this was said with so much rapidity that Pole was hardly able to insert a word of acknowledgment, much less to answer any of Mrs. Steinberg's questions, except, indeed, the one which had reference to his own luncheon; for if he had not assured her that he had eaten two large packets of sandwiches, she would then and there have ordered for him a collation of poached eggs. "Because, dear Mr. Pole," she said, as she glanced at what was being brought in by the servants, "there is absolutely nothing here for you."

She pronounced the word "nothing" with so pathetic an accent of complaint, that Pole looked about, to see what the nothing was. The sight positively overwhelmed him. Whilst he and Mrs. Steinberg had been talking, the corner of the room where they were had undergone a transformation not dissimilar to that which a bare rock undergoes when it is covered by a flock of seagulls. Not only was the tea-table itself laden with butter and toast, but on every table in the neighbourhood had descended some form of food — cakes covered with cream, with almond, with sugar, or with chocolate ; and a plate of Scotch short-bread was reposing on an edition of Dante. " Come," said Mrs. Steinberg, " you really must have something. No ? You won't ? I declare it's too bad of you starving yourself. Well, here is your tea, at all events. Cream ? " she asked. And before waiting for an answer she had given him an allowance so generous as to render his cup undrinkable.

Presently there rose from outside a sound of feminine laughter. " Ah ! " exclaimed Mrs. Steinberg, " there is Ethel at last." And three shortish young ladies, accompanied by a fourth, who was tall, entered the room through one of the open windows.

The shortish young ladies were pretty and pleasant-looking enough, but were all so much alike that it was difficult at first sight to distinguish them. Their clothes, with a humble rashness, aimed at the latest fashion ; their refractory fringes flapped and frolicked upon their eyebrows ; and their laughter rose and fell with a somewhat redundant gaiety. They fell back, however, to make way for the fourth, whose dress, whose bearing, and whose aspect were all singularly different. As soon as she saw Pole she came forward to meet him with a figure whose curves were graceful as those of some tall lily ; and she gave him a welcome—for this was Ethel De Souza—genial as that of her aunt, but subdued, chastened, and ethe-realized. She was, indeed, a woman striking in her whole appearance, not having regular features, but instinct with a noble gracious-ness which showed itself in every movement, and focussed itself in her dark soft eyes ; whilst her voice, equally gracious, had also a pathetic note in it, which made it vibrate with sympathy, and to some ears might have seemed to ask for it.

"I want so much," she said, "to hear about all that has happened to you—about

your place in the country, which I am told
is perfectly beautiful ; and your work, which
I see referred to every week in the papers.
But I won't," she said, dropping her voice,
"ask you about these things now. Bring
up that chair, won't you? And here are the
Miss Cremers—Molly, Dolly, and Folly. I
think you met them once, when you were
staying with us at St. Leonard's."

With an effort, Pole remembered ; and,
indeed, he felt remembrance necessary ; for
the three young ladies, with eyes full of
recognition, were waiting to overwhelm him
with mute reproach, if he did not. The
Miss Cremers were daughters of a half-pay
Indian Colonel, a man well-connected, but,
owing to the narrowness of his means,
reduced to seek for solace, as he approached
the grave, in the sherry, the bitters, and the
billiards that offered themselves to him in
a third-rate yacht-club ; and he was always
delighted, for urgent reasons of economy,
when his daughters were absent from him,
and quartered on some opulent friend. As
for them, they were girls who naturally were
sensible enough, nor were traces of good
birth and breeding ever absent from their
manner ; but they had suffered from their

circumstances. They had not seen much of the world, except the society of the watering-place in which they lived; and the little else which they had seen had hardly been an unmixed advantage to them; for their visits to a few country houses, and an occasional week in London, stimulated them to flavour their conversation with abortive attempts at worldliness, and to excite by an elaborate meekness the criticism which they meant it to disarm. Pole dimly felt all this in the somewhat unnecessary effusion with which, one after another, they all gave him their hands; and the eldest almost directly said to him, with a confidential gentleness, "Mr. Pole, I was staying last week with a mutual friend of ours, Lady Caterham—Jane Caterham. You will be glad to hear that she is quite strong again now, and looking—oh, so beautiful!" As Pole had met Lady Caterham only twice, as he had set her down in his mind as a singularly vuglar person, and had never thought of her since, except when he had refused her invitations, he experienced some difficulty in responding to Miss Cremer's communication. He managed, however, to murmur, with a very creditable show of

interest, " It is a long time since I met her.
I suppose you were staying with her in the
country ? "

"Yes," exclaimed Miss Cremer; "and
such a dear old place it is—what I call a
mellow place—just like Jane herself." And
she was proceeding to describe to him the
glories of its park, its museum, and its ball-
room, when Mrs. Steinberg happily caused
a diversion by asking her niece if " the man
had come about the harp." Miss De Souza
said, " Yes." " Oh," cried the three Miss
Cremers, " dear Mrs. Steinberg, do ask her
to play ! " " Mr. Pole," continued one of
them, looking at him with ecstatic eyes,
" don't you think Ethel on the harp the most
wonderful thing imaginable ? "

"He never has heard me," interposed
Miss De Souza, laughing. " And if he had,
he'd have thought it wonderful only for its
badness."

A sigh of " How can you ? " broke from
the three Miss Cremers ; and Pole, who had
for a moment looked away from them, saw
that they now had seated themselves at
Mrs. Steinberg's feet, holding her hands
coaxingly and caressing her satin knees.
" Oh," they repeated, " do ask her ! "

"Mr. Pole," said Mrs. Steinberg, "these are the dearest girls in the world. I've no doubt, children, she'll play to us after dinner. Don't trouble her now. And listen, I'm sure that one of you will pick Mr. Pole a nice rose for his coat."

"We all will," they exclaimed, and as if by magic they were on their legs again. "Or perhaps, Mrs. Steinberg," said the eldest, "you would like me to find Birkett and get him to show Mr. Pole to his room."

"Molly, dear," smiled Mrs. Steinberg, "that will be very kind of you. Birkett is sure to be in the serving-room lecturing the gardener about the flowers. Indeed, we all must be thinking of going to dress soon. By the way, Mr. Pole," she continued, as he was departing under Miss Cremer's guidance, "to-night we have a treat in store for you. We've an evangelical minister dining here, a friend of Martha Blagdon's. You recollect Mrs. Blagdon, my old school-friend, don't you? She'll be down to dinner. This morning she was a little poorly."

"Over eating!" whispered Miss Cremer to Pole as they left the room.

He was punctual for dinner to a minute, but Mrs. Steinberg was down before him;

and by her side was another lady equally
stout, who, by imitating her dress, was
invested with a superficial resemblance to
her. Before Mrs. Steinberg had uttered a
word of introduction, Mrs. Blagdon, half
rising, and speaking with a solemn huskiness,
said, "I have had the pleasure of seeing
Mr. Pole before. Perhaps he does not
remember an old woman like me. Mr. Pole,
how are you? Are you well? I'm sure you
are looking so." He had taken the fat and
flaccid hand she offered him. It closed on
his like a lobster's claw, and she fastened a
moist glance on him which affronted him
like an unasked-for kiss. Very rarely had he
been more delighted at anything, than he
was at a voice, which freed him from his
present situation—the voice of a servant
announcing Dr. Mogg. Dr. Mogg was a
gentleman with white hair and a stoop, and
a white beard which confused itself with
the crumpled undulations of his shirt. His
shaven upper lip was nearly as spacious as
his forehead, and together, with his mouth,
formed his principal feature. "I'm sure,
ma'am," he said, in response to Mrs. Steinberg's greeting, "I am very happy to have
the honour of dining with you. I've been

blessed for many years with the friendship of Mrs. Blagdon." His natural solemnity was on the present occasion accentuated by a certain shyness; and his mind, which was really busy with the splendour of Mrs. Steinberg's chairs, had given his face an air of unusual thought, when Miss De Souza and her three young ladies entered, and reduced him to a nervous uncertainty as to what to do with his hands. Mrs. Blagdon, however, with the watchful tact of a friend, relieved him of this perplexity by herself taking charge of one of them, and by saying to the Miss Cremers, with a certain chastening tartness, "Well, girls, I hope that this afternoon you have been doing something a little less frivolous than usual." But Miss De Souza had now come to the rescue, and by the magic of her manner she so wrought upon Dr. Mogg that he presently was as much at his ease as he would have been in his own pulpit.

"My dear," whispered Mrs. Blagdon to Mrs. Steinberg, "I know that in fashionable society grace is often forgotten; but I beg you to ask Dr. Mogg to give a blessing."

Mrs. Steinberg nodded, and they presently passed into the dining-room, where the table was gorgeous with flowers and Venetian glass. There Dr. Mogg was given the place of honour, with a *menu* in front of him beginning with two soups, comprising three *entrées*, and ending with Strasburg *pâté*; and just as the Miss Cremers were on the point of seating themselves, Mrs. Steinberg duly asked her reverend companion for a grace. The Miss Cremers straightened their knees; every one remained standing; and for a moment there was a solemn pause, whilst Dr. Mogg considered how he might best improve the occasion. "Oh, Thou," he began at last, clasping his hands before him—"oh, Thou that sittest between the Cherubim, and whose glory is so exceeding that even the Cherubim cover their faces with their wings, consecrate to their appointed use these poor morsels that are before us, and make them humble instruments in the great scheme of our sanctification."

Mrs. Steinberg cast an involuntary glance at her *menu*; the three Miss Cremers appeared to be on the point of tittering; but Pole, who never laughed at any exhibition of religion in the presence of any one who could possibly take it seriously, was pleased at noticing how a look from Miss De Souza's

eyes reduced the young ladies at once to a
state of demure decorum.   As dinner proceeded, indeed, they were quite unable to
refrain from many whispered witticisms as
to the number of poor morsels which found
their way to the lips of Mrs. Blagdon.   But
Mrs. Blagdon, although she occasionally
looked suspicious, was filled by food with a
spirit of Christian gladness that made her
impervious to most worldly annoyances.

"Martha," said Mrs. Steinberg to her,
"you're eating positively nothing.   Don't
pass that jelly.   You'll find it is excellent."

"Thank you, dear," said Mrs. Blagdon,
with an air of meek resignation, and with
two stalactites of cream hanging from her
under lip as she spoke, "don't mind me.   I
assure you I am doing very well.   John,"
she said, turning to the footman, "you may
give me a piece of that, please.   Yes, dear,
this is really good—so well tasted and so
wholesome."   And as she finished it and
returned her spoon to her plate, she looked
round the table, smiling and almost frisky
with content.   "Seeing you all, dear," she
said, turning to Mrs. Steinberg, "has made
me ever so much better than I was.   I think
you are all of you a sight for sore eyes.   I've

had," she continued, with a species of hallowed jauntiness, " a series of blessings since the sun rose this morning — a good breakfast, good friends, a good dinner, and a good day. Do you know, deary, what I did with myself in my bedroom ? I lay on my sofa and read Dr. Mogg's sermons."

" I hope," said Dr. Mogg in slow, rumbling accents, " that those poor words of mine may prove efficacious with souls which need rousing far more than Mrs. Blagdon's. Madam," he whispered, leaning towards Mrs. Steinberg, " might I venture, as I am under an earthly physician's orders, to ask for a glass of brandy, just——" he coughed and paused as if hunting for a sufficiently delicate phrase, "just," he said, " to compose my stomach."

Again the Miss Cremers, who all were remarkably sharp of hearing, were just on the point of indulging in a trio of titters ; nor did Mrs. Blagdon, who regarded them with equal disapproval on account of their worldly minds and their want of worldly goods, tend to calm their risibility by the black looks she cast at them. The situation, indeed, was rapidly becoming strained, and Mrs. Steinberg, who understood it, but was at the same time annoyed by it, became so anxious to get the young ladies into the drawing-room, that she quite forgot to ask for another grace, and left Dr. Mogg, before he had realized what was happening, to the company of Pole and the wine bottles, and the chance, if he cared to use it, of composing a suitable thanksgiving for the benefit of a single auditor.

Pole might, under ordinary circumstances, have found it difficult to entertain so uncongenial a companion; but the way in which that duty had been performed by Miss De Souza — her tender consideration of the old man's feelings and position—had put in his heart an example which he felt constrained to emulate; and Dr. Mogg, though probably regarding him as a brand for that bonfire of the lost, which is for ever to celebrate the triumph and enhance the gaiety of the saved, could not help feeling about him that, judged by human evidence, he was a friendly and kindly gentleman, full of all Christian courtesy. "After you, sir," he said, as Pole opened the drawing-room door for him, the result being that Pole, with a friendly violence, pushed Dr. Mogg forwards, and entered holding him by the arm. As he did this he saw that Miss De Souza was looking at him, and her face, as she did so, brightened with surprised approval.

" Come, Doctor," said Mrs. Steinberg, slapping her sofa, " sit down here, and talk to me and Mrs. Blagdon. Those young people are settling what to play to us. Go, Mr. Pole, and help them."

As Pole approached the group which had clustered about the harp, he found the Miss Cremers apparently fuller than ever of wit and laughter, the zest of which was only intensified by suppression. " Ethel," said one of them, " play him something from Don Giovanni." " No, no," said the second, " Mephistopheles' serenade in Faust." " What will he do ? " said the third. " What effect will it have on him ? I don't suppose he ever heard an opera in his life ;" each of which observations was accompanied by smothered mirth.

" No, no," said Miss De Souza, speaking gently but firmly, and yet accommodating herself to their mood so far as to answer them in a whisper. " Why should we hurt his feelings when he gave us such a delight- ful grace ? Mr. Pole, what shall I play ? Look here—I have thought of these."

" You couldn't," said Pole, " have possibly chosen better."

" Now, girls," said Miss De Souza, " go away and be audience." And seating herself at her instrument, she played with unusual power and feeling, " The Last Rose of Summer," and "Oft in the Stilly Night " ; and, finally, when asked for more she concluded with " Home, Sweet Home."

" Ethel," exclaimed the eldest Miss Cremer when the Doctor had taken his departure, and she and her sisters had again surrounded Miss De Souza, "you ought to be a lion-tamer. Mr. Pole, oughtn't she ? Do you know what Mrs. Blagdon said when you finished the first piece ? She said to Dr. Mogg, in a fat wheezy whisper—no wonder it was wheezy after that disgusting dinner of hers — 'I often think all these talents are a very great snare.' And what do you think he answered ? ' So,' he said, ' are our spiritual talents, unless we employ them properly.' " " One for Martha, that was ! " said the second Miss Cremer, delighted. " And then," resumed the eldest, "when you had finished ' Home, Sweet Home,' there were actually two tears in the good old gentleman's eyes."

"Mr. Pole," said Miss De Souza, lingering at the foot of the stairs, as the rest of the party were going up with their candles. "We haven't had a single word. But I want to thank you for one thing — your kindness to that old man, who must, I am sure, have bored your very life out of you. We shall have a long talk to-morrow, I hope."

"To-morrow," he answered, "I fear I shall have to be away at Windsor. I have told Mrs. Steinberg about it."

"Listen to the clock," she said. "It is only a quarter past ten. The servants hardly ever put out the lights till half-past. Come back with me into the drawing-room and help me to find a book."

He felt her presence affect him as a man with an aching wound is affected by the touch of some cool and healing herb. Every look, every movement of hers was mesmeric with assuaging sympathy. He followed her into the drawing-room.

"You are not," she said, "looking well or in spirits. I hope that all your affairs are going as you could wish them."

"So far as my affairs go," he answered, "everything has been beyond my hopes."

" And you are," she said, "famous already —famous for useful work."

" I could hardly," said Pole, "if I had had the choosing of them myself, have chosen external conditions more favourable than my own ; and I also have done some work which I think is really useful. But I only show—though unhappily I show nobody but myself—how little external conditions are able to ensure happiness. You speak of my work too ; and you think, perhaps, it must give me a good conscience. Let us suppose it does. Let us make that supposition, which so flatters me. But our good consciences do not give happiness to us. Their utmost power as comforters is to help us to bear the want of it."

CHAPTER XIII.

THE following morning Pole received two letters in answer to telegrams he had sent the night before. Both letters were short. The one ran as follows. " My dear Reginald, —Come to lunch or dinner, whichever suits you best. If you do not come at one o'clock, I shall expect you at half-past six. Yours, Randal Bulman." The other was not much longer. " My dear Mr. Pole,—If you please, not luncheon. Come at three, or so soon after as you can. If you don't mind a bad dinner, dine." And there was a signature scrawled so hastily, that had this alone been his guide, it would literally have told him nothing. Reading this last note, he contemplated the careless writing, first with sadness, then with a passing scowl ; and there came into his mind the image of Miss De Souza. He saw before him her face, so sensitive that she seemed to wince at even the passing thought of suffering borne by others. He had noticed her expression as she had asked him after his own welfare, and drawn his confessions from him by the mere magnetism of her sympathy. He recalled it now. He recalled her solicitous kindness towards the old clergyman, and her anxiety to shield him from any accidental mortification; and he said to himself half aloud, "What a strange thing is human nature! Here is one woman, on whom I have no claim whatever, except the claim she gives me by her own natural kindness: and yet she is unhappy at detecting the mere shadow of that suffering which another woman, not only sees with apathy, but inflicts on me without compunction." An hour later, however, when he appeared at breakfast, he was duly arrayed in that garment of calm cheerfulness with which men, in polite society, cover the indecency of sorrow.

"And so," said Mrs. Steinberg, "you are going to lunch with Canon Bulman. There's an account in the paper, I see, of a speech he was making yesterday. And oh!" she exclaimed, taking the paper up, "look at this! They have had their way at last!

Well, I'm very sorry, I confess; and as Martha is not here I can say so."

"Who?" exclaimed the Miss Cremers in chorus. "Dear Mrs. Steinberg, who have had their way?"

"Who? Why, my dears, Canon Bulman and his meddling friends. You know how they have been clamouring that the unhappy man should resign." And she named the political leader who was the object of the Canon's antagonism. "He has not resigned, I see; but two-thirds of his supporters have repudiated him."

"The Canon," thought Pole to himself, as he set off for the station, "will be so full of his triumph, there will really be no holding him." And he managed to divert his mind from other subjects by speculating in the train as to how his host would receive him, and what would be the character of the canonical house and household. As for the house, it was very much what he had foreseen, except that it was a good deal larger. It was Gothic, as Glenlynn was; but yet with a wide difference. The Gothic of Glenlynn — the Gothic of a hundred years ago — was the toy of an aristo-cracy playing at mediæval feudalism. The

Gothic of Canon Bulman's abode, with its
piebald arches of red and yellow brick, was
the toy of a reformed church playing at
mediæval Catholicism.   The building was
divided from the road by a frill of turf only,
and a cast-iron railing, ornamented with
dwarf crosses, over which two excited cats
were vulgar enough to be playing leap-frog.
The pointed windows were white with
muslin curtains, between which were
glimpses of ornaments under glass shades;
and the brass knocker on the varnished
surface of the front door, was so brilliant
that it shone all across the road.   Pole's ring
at the bell was answered by a dark-eyed
parlour-maid, as spruce as the house itself,
but considerably less ecclesiastical.   He, like
Mr. Godolphin, had heard from Dr. Clitheroe,
that the Canon was said to be blind enough
to retain in his service a domestic whose
innocence or whose reformation was by no
means so complete as he believed it to be;
and the moment Pole looked at the young
lady by whom the door was opened, the
Doctor's gossip came back to his mind.   He
gave to her appearance a very cursory attention; but a glance was enough to suggest to
him as an explanation of her presence, that

the Canon, like many of the emotional
apostles of chastity, had a special zeal for
souls which resided in attractive bodies.
This reflection, however, did not occupy him
for a moment, and was quite driven away by
the interior of the Canon's mansion. The hall
was imposing with woodwork of pitch-pine,
scooped and scalloped with various Gothic
devices, which all had a tendency to be more
or less cruciform, and suggestive of sacerdotal
asceticism. The Canon, however, who was
very far from being a sacerdotalist, had
neutralized this effect, by hanging the walls
with magnificent Alpine photographs, photographs of the Cambridge Eight, and engravings of a few crowned heads ; whilst a new
Turkey carpet covered the floor with comfort.
Pole had hardly had time to look round him,
when out came the Canon from a library, and
bid him welcome, with a muscular grasp of
the hand.

"Lunch, Sophie," he said, "as soon as you
can let us have it. And now, Reginald, come
in and see my den. A simple place, this,
but not bad in its way. Look—those rows of
classics—eh—do you remember them? Sit
you down there. You will find that chair
comfortable. Prince Ferdinand was sitting

in that chair last week, and he said he liked it better than anything they could boast of in the Castle."

The Canon, in fact, was in singularly good humour, and that for four different reasons. One was the downfall of the detested and peccant politician; another, the success of his own last evening's eloquence; a third —and perhaps the chief—was the sense that the position of things at Glenlynn was reversed, and that both as a host and a public man he was once again Pole's patron; and the fourth was the pleasure he took in his new house, and especially in displaying its merits to a fresh spectator. And indeed, when Pole reflected that one of the Canon's favourite missions was to lead the crusade of Labour against property, place, and luxury, he could not help feeling that the bitterness of the Canon's spirit was hardly caused by any want of the main advantages which he attacked.

"That," said the Canon, on their way across the hall to luncheon, "is the drawing-room;" and he opened one of the doors and disclosed a spacious apartment, divided in the middle by something like a chancel arch, and fitted with rosewood tables, and albums on bead mats. The Canon was blessed with an exceedingly healthy appetite, but he had neither the grossness of a greedy man, nor any of the refinements of a dainty one; and his table, in these respects, was a very fair reflection of himself. A turbot, a chicken, and an apple tart with cream, followed by a German cheese, the gift of a royal patron—such was the fare he offered; and it was served with appropriate nicety. The silver, though modern, and of very vulgar, inferior design, was plentiful, and well polished; the porcelain plates were adorned with the Canon's monogram; and though the Canon himself took only lemon and soda-water, he provided his guest with a bottle of first-rate claret.

"Well," he said, looking at Pole, with a smile in which the reproving tutor not un-gracefully mixed with the triumphant public man, "you see that I and my friends have had our reward at last, and to our credit as a Christian nation that scoundrel has had to efface himself. I thought, my dear fellow, when I was at Glenlynn, that you treated this and other matters too lightly, or were a little inclined to soften their true features by throwing over them a veil of sentiment—a very tawdry and betinselled veil at the best. I wish, my dear Reginald, you would always beware of sentiment. Next to the absolute temptation of the brute senses themselves, nothing is more dangerous to true and healthy manhood, both in the individual and to society. It does indeed prepare the way for corruption; and it does so by no means more efficacious and fatal than by leading us to judge gently of the sins and of the corruption of others."

"You are not then," said Pole, "of Bunyan's way of thinking, who was accustomed to say, 'If it were not for the mercy of God, I myself should be in that sinner's place!'"

"I am not," said the Canon, giving a slight thump on the tablecloth. "The mercy of God has implanted in us His own image. He has given us eyes to see filth and avoid it; and it is idle to say that we should all of us choose to walk in it unless, besides giving us eyes, He also kept us in leading-strings. If a man chooses to trifle with his own eyesight by putting on his nose the coloured spectacles of sentiment, which will prevent him distinguishing the clean places from the dirty, all I can say is, his dirt be on his own boots; only I don't want his boots to be trampling on my carpet. My dear Reginald, if your friend Bunyan's words mean anything, they mean this—and see how it sounds put this way—If I followed my own inclination I should be a thief, a forger, a murderer, an adulterer, a suicide. In fact it is only by a miracle that I am not one and all of them, as it is. I'm certain that if any one were to say that to either of us we should answer, ' That may be true of you, sir; but I can assure you it is not true of me.' "

It may be inferred that whilst the Canon was discussing these delicate subjects, his two parlour-maids—for the fair Sophie was aided by a sister handmaiden—were not in the room to listen; or, if they were, they were hidden behind a screen, which a hardly audible laugh made Pole think not improbable: and as at this moment their services happened to be requisite, the Canon was obliged to summon them, and give a new turn to the conversation.

It was easy to see, however, that his thoughts had not strayed with his words; for, as soon as his attendants had disappeared, he returned to his previous subject.

"I have," he said, "been doing all I can to encourage football and athletic sports in this neighbourhood. There's no better means of keeping our young men out of temptation. The unlucky thing is, that one gets only at the lower classes. One doesn't get at those which are really the worst offenders—the classes which make these riverside towns the sinks of iniquity they are."

"Indeed!" said Pole. "Are they worse than other places?"

"Oh," said the Canon, "it is deplorable! Artists and men boating—down they come, bringing all the vices of society with them. I tell you, in some of these towns there is hardly a pretty girl who gives you what you can call a really modest look. But that is not the worst of it. All these pretty little villas, looking on the river or hidden away in gardens—these are put to the very worst of purposes. Profligate men take them as summer homes for their mistresses. Wives take them as places where they may meet their lovers. The very Thames itself has become the most immoral river in the world."

The turn of the last phrase almost made Pole laugh; but he composed his muscles, and merely said, "How do you know all this?"

"Ha!" exclaimed the Canon, ironically. "I know, my dear Reginald, because I make it my business to inquire. Some of the landlords of those very villas I was speaking about—God-fearing, clean-minded men; there's one man named Snaggs, especially— a capital fellow, a right-hand man of mine— come to me with pretty stories. I heard from him only yesterday about a woman, who, whatever she is, is not here for any good. But come," he continued, as if ridding his mouth of some nauseous taste—"come, I'll give you one of Prince Michael's cigars. I am sorry to say I have an engagement at three."

Pole was pleased to hear this, as it simplified his own departure; and he could not help smiling, as he bade the Canon good-bye, to think in what a notorious way the giver of these choice cigars was unworthy, on the Canon's principles, to set his boots upon the Canon's carpet. Unwilling to be cross-questioned as to where he was now going, or—more embarrassing still—to be accompanied for any part of the way by his host, he had managed to take his departure when it was hardly half-past two; and, hurrying to the nearest cab-stand, desired to be driven to a house of whose position he knew little, except that it was outside Windsor. When he mentioned the name, the driver seemed well acquainted with it. It lay on the out-skirts of the town ; and Pole, from his slight local knowledge, divined, when the cab turned down a narrow lane, that the river Thames could not be very far away. His conjecture proved correct, and soon between two garden walls he saw a boat flash by on the volume of sliding water. At the same moment the vehicle drew up at a wicket, which bore on its green woodwork the words " Laburnum Lawn."

CHAPTER XIV

POLE dismissed the cab, and pushing the wicket open, entered a pathway, narrow but trimly kept, which went for some dozen yards in a curve between tall bushes. He walked very slowly, as. if shy of emerging from this seclusion, and once or twice he hesitated and stood still. But soon—in a few seconds—the sheltered path had done with him, and he found himself facing a red little brick house, covered with creepers, shining with white window-sills, and looking on a lawn which was studded with brilliant roses, and which opened out by a shy aperture on the stream. In the porch, at the top of some steps, leaning against a pillar, was a woman. When Pole appeared, she at first remained quite motionless, but as he came nearer he saw that her eyes were following him, and her lips were relaxing into a soft gradual smile. Her dress was a blue silk shirt, and a skirt of rough Scotch cloth. In her blue shirt was a rose, and her face was a rose still fresher. Her eyes had the brooding light of a clouded day in June, and in them and on her face, with its soft infantine curves, there rested two expressions —that of the child looking at its mother, and that of a mother looking at her child. When Pole reached the steps, she straightened herself with a little jerk that was half playful in its abruptness, and ran down to meet him ; and her eyes had now in them a faint dancing sparkle which child and mother, when they look at each other, never see. She held out both her hands to him with a frankness that had something timid in it, and looking him earnestly in the face she said, " Are you glad to see me ? " Her voice was singularly sweet, and trembled with a deprecating laugh.

" I think," said Pole, gently and yet sadly, " it is I who should ask whether you are glad to see *me*."

" Yes," she said ; " yes. Of course I am very, very glad."

" I didn't," he answered, " venture to think you would be. But now I look at you, I

really think you are, Pansy. Dear, I believe
you are."

She looked silently at him and merely
nodded her head.

"How pretty," he said, "your garden is,
and the little house, and everything!"

Her face brightened, as if she were glad
to speak of some indifferent subject. "Isn't
it nice?" she exclaimed. "Let us walk
round and see it all. There is an arbour
there, where I thought we would have
tea."

They went together with slow, intermit-
tent paces, pausing now and then to look at
a bush or flower, and only breaking silence
to exchange some trifling observation as to
the name or the beauty of a rose, the neatness with which the place was kept, or
some other obvious topic suggested to them
by the surrounding scene.

"I often," she said, as they came in view
of the river, "sit here, myself quite hidden,
and watch the boats go by. What pretty
spots of colour those men make with their
caps! They row well."

Pole assented, looking vaguely across the
water. Meanwhile she had dropped her
head and was poking at a dandelion with

her parasol. At last he asked if she knew the name of a house, half hidden in trees, on the other side of the water. She seemed for the moment as if she had hardly heard him; and then looking quickly up she uttered the two words, "What, dear?" The unconscious tenderness of her manner, and the way in which the endearing phrase slipped from her, made him turn abruptly round. She raised her eyes to him and his look transfixed her. Half unwillingly she was obliged to return his gaze. "Pansy," he said, "do you know that I think of you night and day? Tell me—do you know it? Dear, have you forgotten everything?"

He spoke low, but his voice shook with suppressed feeling. He did not approach her; but she shrank a little away from him, as a gentle half-tamed animal shrinks from a hand approaching it.

"Don't," she said, "don't—I beg you."

"Don't what?" he asked.

"You know," she replied. "Oh, Reggie, please be kind to me! Be nice and friendly. I haven't too many friends." Then with a light, quick movement she turned away from the river, and said to him, "Come, you have not seen half the garden. And the house—I must show you that—and my books, for I have quite a library.'' She had now summoned to her lips the shadow of a pouting smile. '' You will let me show you my books,'' she said.

Pole's face and bearing showed signs of an internal struggle. His brows contracted, and the lines of his mouth grew harsh. Then, with an obvious effort, he overcame every bitter feeling, and spoke with a voice and smile that answered to her mood. '' Show me,'' he said, ''everything; I am longing to see it all.'' A little childish laugh fluttered amongst her syllables as she answered him. She touched his arm lightly and they went together into the house. There, amongst her books, the conversation came with painless fluency; and if Canon Bulman, in his zeal for the morals of the neighbourhood, had been peering through the window and had known nothing of either, he might have thought them brother and sister, or cousins who had long been separated. It is true that Pole, when her face was turned from him, sometimes looked at her with a wondering and half-pitying sadness; but he continued to laugh pleasantly, and talk to her with tranquil sympathy, as if intercourse such as this left no emptiness in his heart.

Meanwhile time had gone by quickly, and a maid now appeared at the door of the room where they were sitting, and said that tea had been taken into the arbour. "Will you," said his hostess to him as they rose, "bring out a book with you and read to me? Any one you like—Shelley, or that volume of Dickens."

He did as she bade him with a slight reluctant sigh, and slowly followed her out of doors. When they sat down in the arbour he was silent and his face was changed.

"Have I bored you," she said, "with talking about myself? I have! I know I have, and now you are going to hate me! But, Reggie, I've no one but you to whom I can tell my thoughts; and when I see you they all come pouring out; and lately, until I came here, I have had no time for thinking."

"May I," he said, "ask what has been occupying you?"

"Oh," she replied, "every kind of thing— practical things. You've no idea what a house the castle is; and everything comes on me. I shall have to work like this for

another twenty years at least. Perhaps,"
she said gently, "you will be able to see
now why I so seldom have time to write to
you. You wouldn't wish me—would you?—
to neglect my duties. You ought rather to
encourage me to do them."

Whilst she spoke he looked straight before
him, as if he did not hear her. She might
have seen by the movement of his throat
that he was agitated by some emotion. At
last he said in a low, deliberate voice—

"It is right. You must do the duties that
are claiming you on every side. Your new
life—the life you have so gladly chosen—
must take you and make you part of itself,
surround you and absorb you, and raise you,
and change you past my knowing you; and,
better still, it will change you so that you
will have no need of me." His voice, as he
went on, had acquired a growing bitterness,
and there was something in it almost fierce
as, turning on her abruptly, he said to her,
"Is not that so?"

She looked at him with a face that was
frightened rather than angry, and bewildered
rather than frightened.

"Dear," she exclaimed, "don't be rough
with me!"

Those few helpless words in an instant disarmed his anger.

"Forgive me," he said; "do I ever wish to wound you?"

"No!" she answered. "No; you don't. Be kind and good, then, and read to me."

He took the book up and began to turn its pages; but as he did so, his eyes kept straying towards the tea-tray.

"What is it?" she asked.

"I was looking at the cups," he said. "I see there are only two. I thought those little cakes might perhaps be for some one else. Is no one else here, Pansy?"

She slowly shook her head. "There was," she replied, "but they both of them went to London this morning. They went with nurse, to see the doctor."

Again his face darkened, but he spoke quite equably.

"Come," he said, "I will read now. Here is a chapter that always made you laugh. I could hardly trust myself to utter my own thoughts."

These last words were muttered rather to himself than her, and he began his reading without more ado. He read well, and with apparent interest and willingness; and she, as she listened, kept her eyes fixed on him, and laughed encouragingly at every amusing passage. But in time it seemed as if he were wearying of some painful effort. The spirit went from his voice; his elocution became monotonous; and at last she stopped him, saying—

"You're not attending; no, not the least bit. You've made three mistakes in those last two sentences. There, put your book down and talk to me. We have read enough."

He put the book down with alacrity, and abruptly asked her a question which, to judge from his manner, had been in his mind some time.

"Why," he said, "would you not let me come to luncheon?"

"I couldn't," she said; "I was expecting the dressmaker, so if you had come earlier you would hardly have seen anything of me. Why do you laugh like that?"

"I was smiling," he replied, "at a picture which what you have said suggested to me —a picture of you holding a pair of scales, with a man's soul in one, and some new petticoats in the other."

"No, no," she said, trying to laugh lightly.

" Your soul was not at stake, only your body. And I do hope that you managed to get lunch somewhere."

He told her he had.

"Where was it?" she asked gently. "Where did you have your lunch, dear? Won't you tell me?"

He answered brusquely. " In Windsor, at Canon Bulman's. He was my tutor once."

"Oh," she said, "the man who makes all those speeches? Very well, and what did Canon Bulman talk about?"

"Oh," replied Pole, "he talked about his usual topic. If you very much want to know, he talked about the virtue of chastity. He thinks a man who has lost it is very nearly as bad as a woman." Pole would have been seen by any careful observer to have been speaking at random, and to have been hardly conscious of a listener; but there was in his tone a certain contemptuous bitterness that gave his words an edge, although they were uttered absently.

Her lips parted with a hardly audible gasp, and her face appeared to be frozen with some sudden and uncomprehended pain. " I don't think," she faltered at last, "that you ought to say things like that to me." She paused and bit her lip, and her cheeks became slowly crimson. "It is not delicate," she said, getting out the words with difficulty. Then all at once her eyes filled with tears, and hastily rising from her seat, she stamped on the gravel with her feet, and turning her back on him she hid her face in her handkerchief. "It's too bad of you," she exclaimed in broken tones. "What did you mean by that? Did you mean anything? How dare you come down here and talk to me like this!"

"Pansy," exclaimed Pole, distressed beyond measure at this outburst, and at first bewildered as to the cause of it. "What have I said? You know I never meant to pain you."

But without noticing his question she began to walk away from him. "I am going," she said, "into the house."

"Shall I come too?" he asked humbly.

"As you like," she said, without turning her head. But a moment later, throwing him a glance over her shoulder, "No," she added, "you had better not. Go away—you had better go."

Instead, however, of accepting his dismissal, he rose, and unchecked followed her

with deliberate steps. They presently found
themselves once more in the drawing-room.
As they entered, he closed the door. The
slight sound made her turn round and look
at him. " You needn't shut it," she said. " I
am not going to stay here. I'm only looking
for a book; I am then going up to my bedroom." And she began to examine the books
with an attempt at ease and indifference,
though her eyes, had he only observed them,
were not in a condition to see. She took up
a book at hazard, and began moving towards
the door. " I am going upstairs," she said
coldly; " will you kindly let me pass ? "

" No," he said, with a hard determination
that startled her. " I will not let you go till
you hear what I have to say." She tried to
laugh, as if in that way she might conciliate
him, but the little sound she emitted was
hardly audible. At all events he did not
heed it. " Pansy Masters," he continued,
grasping her tightly by the arm, " I order
you to go back. Go ! Sit down in that
chair. Whatever happens, by God, I will be
heard ; and you shall not leave me taking a
false impression." By this time she had
obeyed him ; she had seated herself in the
chair helplessly. At the sound of his oath,

she winced as if he had struck her with a horsewhip. "I see," he said, struggling to speak calmly, "I see now what you fancied, when I spoke about Canon Bulman. But when I spoke I was not thinking of you. You had driven me back on myself, and I was thinking — I was thinking — of many things. Do you imagine for a moment I was such a coward, such a brute, such a fool, as to apply to yourself anything that the Canon said to me? The Canon! My thoughts were busy with him for a very different reason. He talks about chastity. He has no idea what the word means. St. Francis preached to birds. I don't know if he ever tried pigs. The Canon's ideas of virtue are those of a converted pig. When I spoke to you just now, I was contrasting in my own mind what he would teach me with what I have been taught by some one else. Some one else has taught me to feel in my heart of hearts the holy and living thing that this virtue really is—to feel that, in its highest form, it is no refusal or negation, but the self-devotion of body and soul at once—of the reasonable soul and flesh that is one man. Chastity is the complete living of one human being for another, which is merely

the humanized form of the Saints living for
God. And who has taught me this? Who
has opened my eyes? It is you — you.
Pansy, do not you know that? Have I loved
you so long in vain—to such little purpose?
It was for you I exiled myself all those years
in Germany; for you that I—— Ah, but I
can't speak of it. The thought of you has
been always with me." He paused; his
voice trembled, and sitting down by her, he
leant his face on his hand. "Pansy," he
said, "I can't describe it. You have been a
presence always dwelling in me, softening all
my hard thoughts and quickening all my
good ones, and giving my soul wings, and
enabling me to forget self. And now, what
do you do?" he exclaimed with returning
bitterness. "I had not much to give you;
but all that I had I gave; and you have taken
it all—all—everything in me out of which
happiness might have been made. And you
—you leave me with as little compunction as
if I had been an upper servant. For six
months you never write a single line to me—
although, Pansy, there are such things as
mails between England and America; and at
last when you do write, it is only a careless
word or two. I could bear that, if your

unkindness ended there. But does it? Think. I travel two hundred miles for the sole purpose of seeing you. Of the few hours we might spend together, you give up three to your milliner; and of the hours we have actually spent, you take up the larger part in gossiping about the monthly reviews, and making me read Dickens to you. I have tried to speak to you—the real you; but in vain. You elude me, you repulse me. You treat me as some stranger, whom you had seen for the first time yesterday. And there is something else I had wished and hoped to see; and you—you deny me that! You have no heart; but do you think that I have none? or that it is made of wood or leather? Perhaps I had none once; but you have given me one, and you are murdering it! Woman," he exclaimed, "how can you treat me like this? Do you realize what relation I am to you?—what link must always bind me to you?"

All this while she had sat in the chair motionless; but at these last words she rose with her face rigid, and stumbling forward a step or two, abruptly stood still and faced him. "When you speak like that," she said, in a low constrained voice, "I hardly know where to turn. How can you? I will not submit to it. Oh! I hate you!" She remained looking at him with an expression that seemed to repeat her language; but as she did so her eyes suddenly filled with tears again. A little gasp broke from her. She felt feebly and in vain for her handkerchief; and then approaching him with a curiously natural movement, she took his from the breast of his coat, and she convulsively pressed it to her eyes. A second later she hid her face on his shoulder, her hands clutched his sleeve, and he felt her sobs shaking him.

They dined together like friends; but their manner was so subdued and quiet, that a listener could hardly have conjectured the precise terms on which they stood. "And I may then," he said at parting, "see you again before I go?" She replied in a half whisper, "The day after to-morrow. And I will—indeed I will—try to be better to you, and to write oftener. I ought to—I owe you every-thing. Dear, good night." His lips touched her, and he was gone.

CHAPTER XV

HE returned to Thames Wickham oppressed by a profound melancholy, his heart reproaching him with the hard language he had used, yet bruised and wounded itself by the treatment he had just received. " All my hopes," he said to himself, " are over. She has no wish to pain me. She has lost almost all sense that it is in her power to do so. Yes," he continued, " I am nothing to her; and except her, no one is anything to me. Will she ever know—never! how should she ?—what I am doing for hers, if not for her ? " Then again his imagination confronted him with the image of Miss De Souza; and the thought of her sympathy, as contrasted with the cruel heedlessness of another, embittered his mind afresh, and yet at the same time soothed it.

It was late when he reached Mrs. Steinberg's, and his friends had retired to bed; but

the following morning at breakfast, he
received the welcome news that the three
Miss Cremers were going for the day to
London; and Miss De Souza, as soon as
they had taken their departure, asked him if
he would like to come for a little row on the
river. "And we might," she said, "rest
somewhere under a bank, and talk." He
fetched his hat—she had hers on already—
and they went out together into the garden.
"How different," he thought, "is the treatment I am meeting now from that which I
met with in that other garden yesterday!"
And a short involuntary sigh reached his
companion's ear.

Before them was a lawn sloping down to
the Thames. It was shaded with old cedars
and traversed by broad walks. Beds of
geraniums glittered in appropriate places.
There were steps of white stone, and bright
coloured majolica vases, and a tribe of
luxurious chairs with plump red cushions
under the trees. Close to a landing-place
was one of the gardeners waiting, with a boat
in readiness — a boat light but roomy,
cushioned as luxuriously as the chairs and
built for indolent drifting.

"We shan't want you, Walter," said Miss

De Souza, as they embarked. "How is your wife? Is she better? I hope she liked the jelly that I made for her yesterday. This afternoon, if she will let me, I will come and read to her. That man's poor wife," she explained to Pole when he dipped his sculls into the water, and they glided out into the stream, "has a terrible internal complaint. It relieves her sometimes being read to."

A better means of leading to unreserved conversation and of gathering up the threads of an old and intimate friendship, could not have been devised than an expedition like this. For the little discussions that were necessary as to where they should best go, together with the physical occupation which fell to the lot of one of them, enabled them, by easy degrees and without any abrupt transition, to pass from the subjects which lie on the surface of life, to those which are hidden beneath and which conversation rarely reaches.

"Your aunt," said Pole, alluding to a conversation which had taken place at breakfast, in the course of which Mrs. Steinberg had indulged in some vigorous language, "was very severe on Canon Bulman, and all his splendid speeches. And yet he's a man who has many excellent qualities."

"I," said Miss De Souza, "confess I have no patience with him. I could hardly read the speech which he made at Reading. But then, perhaps, I am prejudiced, and I have a reason for being so."

"I was not aware you knew him," exclaimed Pole with some surprise.

"No more I do," she answered. "But I used to know his wife. Poor woman, I pity her."

"His wife!" Pole ejaculated. "Do you mean to tell me he is married? How? when? where? I have known him for fourteen years; though, no doubt, there have been long intervals during which I have lost sight of him. Do you mean he has a wife alive?"

"His wife," said Miss De Souza, "was the daughter of a Cambridge surgeon. He married her on being presented to a living, when he resigned his Fellowship. Ten years ago this was. They were only together for a year; and then they agreed to separate. There was nothing wrong, as people put it with so much unconscious irony—as if what they call wrong were not of all wrongs the least. 'He was always preaching,' she said to me, 'about people saving their souls. He never treated me as if I had a soul at all.'"

"Where did you know her?" asked Pole.

"Abroad," said Miss De Souza, "at a little place in the Pyrenees. I often think of one thing she said to me. 'I shouldn't so much have minded had there been other women in the case. I could forgive him for having broken my heart; but I cannot forgive him for having hardened it.' And then," Miss De Souza continued, "I must tell you one more thing. It will show you the sort of terms they were on. 'You are always flattering yourself,' Mrs. Bulman once said to him, "that you are not as other men are. It is lucky for the happiness of women that most men are not as you.'"

"It's odd," said Pole, "I should never have heard of this; but of course it is a thing he would keep as quiet as he could. What made him marry the woman, I wonder?"

"I should think, from what she told me," said Miss De Souza, "that on one side of his character, he was just the man to be taken by a pretty face. By the way, I ought, however, to mention this in his favour—that he made her, considering his means, a very handsome allowance. She died last year. I saw her death in the papers."

"And now, I suppose," said Pole, "her allowance comes back to the Canon. His fine new house must be more or less a memorial to her."

By this time they were opposite the mouth of a quiet stream which came floating into the river by many curves and elbows, and formed, under an arch of foliage, an avenue paved with water.

"Shall we go up there," said Miss De Souza, "and stay quiet under the willows?"

He assented; and before long they were stationary in a shady place.

"How hot it must have made you," she said, "rowing in that burning sun! Lie down and be comfortable. There are any number of cushions."

The stern of the boat, indeed, was like an oriental divan, alluring the mind, through the body, to placid dreaming and meditation; and for some time they neither of them opened their lips, except for some broken remarks on the sound of the water or the reflections in it, or the summer sky, which showed itself in dancing tesselations between the leaves.

At last Pole said, "I hope that I have not been speaking of the Canon too hardly. To speak bitterly of any one leaves a bitter taste in the mouth."

"Yes," said Miss De Souza. "I know how you feel that. You did not when first I knew you; at all events, not so keenly."

"That," he said, "is because as one lives on, one learns how little one could stand hard judgment one's self. But as for the Canon, in spite of what you say about his wife, there is only one thing in him which I really dislike personally. I mean those opinions on which he happens most to value himself."

"Canon Bulman to me," said Miss De Souza, "represents an idea of virtue which has caused far more misery than most men's lapses into vice. His own wife's history is an instance of this. You see, I speak as a woman; and I have known — well, only a few weeks since, I was seeing a friend of mine—such a noble, patient woman, whose heart, from morning to night — I do not exaggerate—never ceases aching. And why? On account of a husband who, because he does not ill-treat her in one way, thinks himself at liberty to ill-treat her in every other. He neglects her, he wastes her money, he has never a tender word for her. Oh! men never can know how a woman can be made to suffer by a husband whom our Canon Bulman would compliment as a model of fidelity. If a man loves you, and is what is called unfaithful, you can forgive him and take him back to you. If he does not love you, if his warmth is coldness, if his light is darkness, you have nothing of value either to lose, or to win back, or to keep. It has always seemed to me that to call a man a good husband because he does not do one particular thing, is as wise as to call him a good husband because he happens not to be a smuggler. I hope, Mr. Pole, you're not shocked at me for talking like this."

He watched her. Her voice was trembling, and her eyes, which were turned away from him, and were looking up at the whispering movement of the leaves, had in them the strained, and almost painful intentness by which alone eyes sometimes are kept dry. "Does," she continued, "what I say sound unchristian? I am a Christian;

I say my prayers. I am not married, and I never shall be. These questions personally do not affect me ; but they affect me through the way in which I have known them affect other women, and instinctively I know that in their place I should have felt the same. Please do not think—indeed, I am sure you will not—that I make light of that which is commonly called virtue : but in man, and even in woman, it seems to me mainly beautiful—how shall I put it ?—as a sign of something else, as the blush which the heart sends to the cheek of a deeper constancy."

" You asked me," said Pole, " a minute ago, if I thought what you said unchristian. Who are the women whose faces shine at us from the pages of the gospel ? Of course there is the sacred Mother, and Mary, the sister of Lazarus. But who are the others ? They are Mary Magdalene, the woman of Samaria, and the woman taken in adultery. If you are wrong," he went on, " I should say you were wrong because your view of things is too high, rather than too low. You can understand only the nobility of the flesh. Canon Bulman can understand only its vileness."

For a time they were silent. At last he resumed, in a different tone—

"You say that you yourself feel strongly about these matters, because the confidences of two women have shown you their practical bearing. I am not married, and, like you, I never shall marry; so, like you, as far as that goes, they do not concern me personally. But, like you, I have had strange things brought under my notice. One was brought under my notice the other day, and it has been in my mind all the time we have been talking."

"Is it anything," said Miss De Souza, "that you could tell me?"

"All I can tell of it," said Pole, "doesn't sound much when told. It is only a little story which I conjecture or divine to be taking place at this moment. A man of whom I knew something—this is the long and short of it—became connected three or four years ago with a married woman, who had been practically deserted by her husband. The man was devoted to the woman, and gave up everything for her; and she, too, was devoted in the most passionate way to him. Well, the lady's husband, who was at first very much out at elbows, has since come into a considerable family property, and now has induced his wife to go back and live with him. Of course, there are a thousand reasons why she should do so. An avenue is open to her full of interests and duties, and no doubt she sees her soul saved respectably at the end of it. But, of course, to walk in this avenue with comfort, it is necessary that she should get rid of her lover. She won't want to have him jumping out of the bushes and joining her; and the process of getting rid of him is what she is now most intent upon. He's not a man who would for a moment keep her against her will. He would probably urge her to take the very course she is taking. But the curious question is, what will he think of her past relations with himself, when he sees how easily she can sever them? What will he think of the value of her love for a new life, when it costs her hardly a pang to say good-bye to the old? Will he think that her soul is more likely to be saved because she hastens to save it with such very little compunction?"

"Oh!" exclaimed Miss De Souza, "but a woman *must* feel under such circumstances. She couldn't do as you say, if she ever really had cared for him. She would only deserve happiness, she would only deserve peace, in proportion to the misery she felt in seeking for them without her friend. Why, a woman such as you describe is a woman who would, if she were ship-wrecked, cling to a swimmer till she was picked up by a boat, and then leave him to drown, exhausted by his toil in saving her."

"Women," said Pole, "are always hard on women. I felt angry at the thought of her when first I heard the story. But women are weak—so are men too—and life is hard ; and whenever I think of complicated cases like this I am inclined to cut the knot —though I am not a Christian like you—by saying, " 'God have mercy on us, for we all of us need mercy ! ' "

He said these last words simply, and yet they dragged a little in their utterance, as if he were unaccustomed to this species of confession. For a time they were both silent. Then he said, " It does one good to talk to you. I am not going to compliment you on all the wise things you say. I am thinking of the way you affect me, not by what you say, but by what you are. I find myself expressing to you easily, without false shyness, things which very often I can hardly acknowledge to myself. Your presence thaws thoughts in me which generally are cold and frozen."

"If that is so," she said, "it is only because, being so weak myself, I feel doubly the troubles of stronger minds. It touches me that you should be troubled—you who are so much above me in every way."

"Ah," he said lightly, "if I am to go on telling the truth to you, you must never yourself say things so far from the truth as that."

When they reached the house again the midday post had arrived, and Pole found a letter for him lying on the hall table. The well-known, untidy writing brought the blood to his face.

"My dearest Reggie," it ran, "I am suddenly obliged to leave. I must go to-morrow, and shall not come back again. I am very busy to-day, and have hardly a spare moment; but come here this afternoon —about four o'clock, if possible—and see Pansy just for a few minutes. Dear, I am yours.

"Pansy."

His brain, as he read, was confused by a rush of thoughts, reproachful recollections amongst them of things which he had said in the boat whilst this letter was actually on the way to him. The gong for luncheon was sounding. He hurried upstairs to his room, and ringing for his servant sent him off with a telegram, containing the words, "Punctually at four o'clock."

He excused himself for his absence to Mrs. Steinberg—not a very difficult matter, as she took it for granted that he was going to London for an hour or so; and he found himself, at the time appointed, again in the narrow lane which led between the garden walls and the gate of Laburnum Lawn. When he was still too far off for the actual wicket to be visible, he fancied he saw some movement at the opening in which the wicket was. "Can it," he thought, "be possible that I shall find other visitors with her?" This fear was still in his mind when a movement was again apparent, and in another moment a figure emerged into the lane. It was her own. With a shy slow-ness, which yet had something that was eager in it, she advanced towards him. "Pansy," he said to himself, "how have my doubts been wronging you!" They met. There was a smile on her face like the flickering light that is reflected from water. It was tremulous with the affection of which her eyes were full. As he took her hand a tenderness filled his heart, like that felt by a man for a little helpless bird which has fallen from its nest and is too young to fly; and there broke from him, in a low tone, many of those terms of endearment which, when recorded, are colourless, or even ridiculous, but which, in the air of passion, have a life as vivid and beautiful as the sea anemone has in its own world of waters.

They went into the garden together. She told him all her plans. She explained the reasons of her departure, which he saw was both necessary and unwilling, due as it was to some difficulty with the servants in her new home; and then they stood almost silent, bending over a yellow rose, as if its scent and colour were a parting thought which they were sharing.

Presently she said, " I told you that I had my step-child with me. She is very kind to me now, and I hope I do all I can for her. But there is something else here which

I must show you. Wait for me, and I will be back directly."

With a naïve, girlish gesture she ran across the lawn and into the house, and Pole could hear her voice calling out to somebody. Indistinctly the sound of an answer reached him, with another sound following this, pitched in a higher key; and then his companion reappeared in the doorway, and slowly descended the steps, leading a little boy. If the child of a woman he had never seen before had been enough to attract him as it played before the moorland cottage, much more was he attracted by the apparition now before him. He went towards it; he lifted it in his arms for a moment; and he and its mother led it between them to a seat.

"Take him," she said, "on your knee;" and they listened to it, watched, and talked to it.

It was a pretty child, affectionate to almost a premature degree, and the spirit of childhood laughed in its dark eyes like a star through a night of melancholy. The mother's gaze wandered from it to Pole, and, without saying a word to him, her hand grasped his. The child's presence, however, insured them against silence. The seat, thanks to it, was a centre of conversation and laughter. But this did not avail to drown the notes of a chiming clock, which caused the boy's mother to look at her watch and start.

"A quarter to five!" she exclaimed. "Dear, you must go; I can't stay with you longer. And here in the garden I can't even say good-bye to you—at least, I can only say it. But," she said, "I'll tell you what I will do. He and I will walk part of the way up the lane with you."

Slowly and reluctantly they both rose and went, the mother gently leading her little boy, and saying to Pole, "You take his other hand."

"And you will," said Pole, as they passed through the garden gate, "write to me, Pansy, sometimes, and not make me feel that you have forgotten me, though I never will ask of you to think of me in any way which you feel to conflict with the life which you wish to lead."

"Yes, dear, I will write," she said. "I will not be unkind again. But don't look so sad. You will frighten him; he is watching you."

Pole stooped down to the small figure between them. "Dear, dear little man," he

said, " I wouldn't frighten you for the world ;
and when I think of you I shall be kind to
every little boy I see." He had just pressed
his lips on the diminutive upturned face,
when the mother exclaimed, " Reggie, there
is some one coming. We must go back,
dear. Say good-bye to us, and we must
go."

He again embraced the child ; he wrung
the mother's hand ; and as she turned away
she hastily kissed the tips of her fingers to
him. He was on the point of casting a last
glance behind him, when he realized that a
pedestrian was already advancing down the
lane. The new-comer was a man with a
confident, swinging gait. He twirled his
stick as he walked ; his head was well thrown
back ; his muscular lips gripped each other.
A gold watch-chain and a gold cross gleamed
on him. Pole saw with a start that the
stranger was Canon Bulman.

For a moment Pole and the Canon stared
at each other in silence.

" Ah," said Pole at last, " so you see me
again in Windsor. I have just come over for
an hour to call on an old friend."

" Your friend," said the Canon, " it appears,
has been able to work a miracle and combine

in her own person the charms both of age and youth." These words, which were accompanied by a certain inquisitorial scrutiny, converted the embarrassment, from which Pole was suffering, into resentment, and supplied him with resolution to cut short the interview.

"I, at all events," he said coldly, "have no miraculous powers, so I must not wait a moment, or else I shall miss my train."

END OF VOL. I.

PRINTED BY WILLIAM CLOWES AND SONS, LIMITED,
LONDON AND BECCLES.

www.ingramcontent.com/pod-product-compliance
Lightning Source LLC
Chambersburg PA
CBHW030631030726
47497CB00006B/1742